Acknowledgements

To all of my support base that voted for this to be my next project.

Thanks to Sarah Barnes, Matthew Brown, Christopher Hubble, Sarah Dawes, Todd Barnes, Hayden Rowley, Adam Storoschuk, Rebecca Harris, Mark Smith, Damian Hill, Anna Hubble, Pete Stevens & Charles Raymond.

Thanks to Sarah for naming the Sheriff.

MAPLE FALLS
MASSACRE

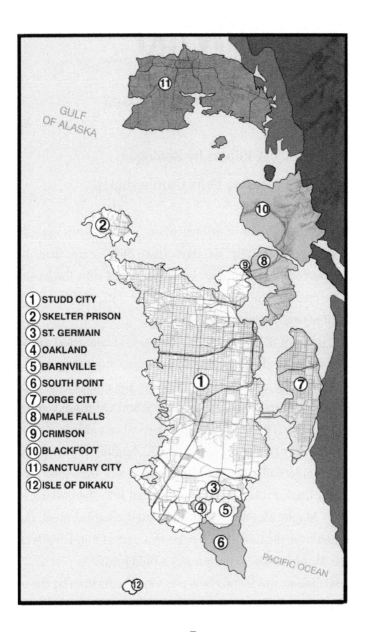

GULF OF ALASKA

1 STUDD CITY
2 SKELTER PRISON
3 ST. GERMAIN
4 OAKLAND
5 BARNVILLE
6 SOUTH POINT
7 FORGE CITY
8 MAPLE FALLS
9 CRIMSON
10 BLACKFOOT
11 SANCTUARY CITY
12 ISLE OF DIKAKU

PACIFIC OCEAN

CHAPTER I

Does The Blackfoot Exist?

A Report by Zoologist,
Professor Felix Cumberbatch

It was the middle of winter when I started my expedition, which took approximately six days (two days more than I had initially expected). I have always been fascinated with the legendary tales of the creature known as Sasquatch (or Yeti, Bigfoot or indeed The Blackfoot) and its legitimacy.

When the Dean of SCU (Studd City University) contacted me about the possibility of doing a lecture to his students about the authenticity of such a creature, I jumped at the chance. For I, could not with my hand on my heart stand there and tell those youngsters that it did not exist, because nobody has ever been able to declare its existence one way or the other. With SCU funding my expedition I set off for Maple Falls, Blackfoot territory. I was incredibly excited on that very brisk Friday evening as I pulled into the parking lot of The Fallen Maple Motel, a tired and dated establishment that is situated just over the Canadian border in a part of Maple Falls called Downtree. It is here where my journey would begin.

The establishment was owned by a pleasant ageing man by the name of Kit Ulrich. Oh how he laughed when I told him of my plans for the week, he even had tears streaming down his gaunt face from the hysterical fit I'd put him in, all by the mere mention of the word, Yeti. He handed me a welcome pack and my key while wiping the tears from his shallow sockets with the back of a liver spotted hand and shook his head.

"Boy, you must be out of your mind!" He chuckled calming himself back down, before asking "And who you going out there with? Not on your lonesome?"

I informed him that tomorrow morning I would be liaising with a Mr Muchnick, a cryptozoologist and a resident of the Maple Falls area and an apparent aficionado on the Yeti species.

Well, you would have thought that I had just told Mr Ulrich the funniest joke that he had ever heard, because the seams on his sides split and he spat in a fit of hysterics, the tears running again only being stopped from reaching his chapped lips by his bushy greying moustache.

"Chuck? 'Crazy' Chuck Muchnick!" He screamed thumping his fist down relentlessly on the guestbook, where only moments ago I'd scribbled my signature. Now with each thud smudging my fine penmanship into an indecipherable splurge.

I smiled and took my key that he held out in his shaking palm, his legs now crossed as he shook as if any second now his bladder would lose all control and empty its contents into the front of his underpants.

I didn't feel like any supper as I lay in bed watching shadows dance across the ceiling. Besides, the Transylvanian Nightmare Combo that I'd eaten that afternoon while driving through Crimson was enough to fill me up, and in all honesty I had no appetite.

7

I struggled to sleep that night in room 7 of The Fallen Maple Motel. An amalgamation of excitement, fear and trepidation filled by head, making sleep impossible. I felt like a child going out on some great adventure, and in some ways I guess I was.

But as the wind whipped ice and snow against a window that was consumed by condensation, I found myself focusing on one thing Mr Ulrich had said, 'Crazy' Chuck Muchnick.

Crazy.

The word crazy danced around my head and made the pit of my stomach gurgle in nervousness.

What if this man was crazy? But surely the university wouldn't have set me up with some fruitcake would they? Surely not, was the only thing I could keep reiterating to myself but in all honesty, it did nothing to douse my fears.

Saturday morning was bright and fresh and as I'd finished spitting toothpaste into the bathroom's basin there was a knock at the door. I froze for a second, Crazy Chuck I thought, and wiped excess minty paste from my lips with a hand towel that had a small red maple leaf embroidered into its corner. The knock came again. I told myself I was being silly as I crossed the small room towards the door. But as I reached for the cold metal doorknob, I stopped myself. What if he was some axe murderer! I swallowed hard and the sound of my descending gulp seemed to reverberate off the walls. I shook my head and chuckled at the absurdity of such a thought, and composing myself, I opened the door.

The first thing I noticed was that I was face to face with the shining dark eyes of a racoon. So startled by such a greeting I teetered backwards slightly on my heels, swaying for a split second before I managed to grasp the door and steady myself.

I soon realised it was in fact a harmless hat, some roadkill or hunting prize that had been turned into wintery headgear, and not some feral racoon pouncing at my face looking to gouge my eyes from their sockets.

I looked down to see who was hiding under such a garish bonnet and a small man with the widest eyes, the wide eyes of excitement, that seemed almost childlike, glared back at me. I found myself lost for words and just stared at him. Then through a layer of heavy stubble he shot me a toothless grin.

"Pro-fessor Grumble-patch?" He asked.

I smiled and corrected him that it was in fact Cumberbatch and shook his heavily gloved hand. I told him he could call me Felix and he smiled again chewing on something brown and gooey, it looked to have the consistency of tar or treacle, but I knew in fact it was tobacco and cringed with the notion that even nowadays people would still partake in such pastimes.

"Chuck!" He sniffed as he introduced himself, tobacco seeping down his chin, but then was quickly wiped away with the sleeve of his already heavily stained yellow, fur trimmed Parker.

We tackled the three hour drive towards Maple Woods in Chuck's beaten up 1982 Chevrolet 4x4 pick up. The truck itself filled me with a strange case of nostalgia, my memory banks conjuring up old episodes of *The Fall Guy*, which I used to thoroughly enjoy when I was a youngster. I was apprehensive whether the old ramshackle would be able to make the journey, but I was assured that this wasn't the truck's first rodeo.

Was Chuck crazy? Probably... I mean he was off galavanting around the Canadian wilderness every weekend looking for Sasquatch so I guess he has to be, right? Well, that's exactly what I am doing too! So that would mean I'm crazy too. But all joking aside, no, I don't think he's crazy, a little eccentric and enthusiastic, but not crazy.

I'd summarise it by saying that he is misunderstood by the residents of Maple Falls, he believes in something and is passionate about it, just because it's different from the thoughts and beliefs of the majority, doesn't make it wrong.

Chuck Muchnick is a fountain of knowledge and information, what he doesn't know about Maple Falls & Blackfoot isn't worth knowing.

He told me about how this was not the middle of winter as I'd believed, not in Maple Falls anyway, this was mild for the area, he told me that you knew when the winter was truly here by the water. The rivers, creeks and lakes that amass in this part of the world, freeze up. That's when you know it's winter in Maple Falls.

"It'll be cold enough to freeze the balls off a cougar." Chuck said between chewing and slurping as we made our way up Maple Drive, which was the main access road up to the town. We passed hardly any vehicles on the way, and we were sandwiched on our journey by masses of redwoods on either side for almost the entire journey, beautiful and picturesque, but daunting. To see their sheer gargantuan size swaying from side to side in the wintery breeze was enough to make your bladder quiver.

"The Maple River freezes first, then that son of a bitch of solid ice works its way up to Old Syrup." Chuck told me.

'Old Syrup' was the Maple Lake or as it was called in the days of the Natives 'The Great Maple Lake'. In fact the whole area was once called Great Maple and not Maple Falls at all. It was playfully referred to as 'Old Syrup' as a play on the condiment Maple Syrup, so Maple Lake became Maple 'Syrup' Lake.

He also told me about Tear Drop Creek.

"Now, Tear Drop Creek, that's what the Indians called it. As the story goes, some heartbroken Indian girl lost her baby in that creek and cried and cried for the longest of time on its banks. They say t'was her tears that filled the son of a bitch!" He laughed at the sheer ridiculousness of the tale "Isn't that the damnedest piece of horse shit you ever heard?"

I found the comparison to Chuck and the Native Indians beliefs humorous. Here he was laughing about the traditional tale, or myth, but then chasing the woods looking for another type of myth.

"Tear Drop rises up through Talon, Cross and Maple, before joining Old Syrup."

It was around then that he opened a bag of salted peanuts and drove a rough dirty hand into the share size bag, before stuffing them into his greasy maw. He offered me some but I declined, the only positive about watching him eat those peanuts was that the strong aroma of salted nuts had managed to suppress the damp musky smell of that damn racoon that sat proudly on his head. It may have well been a skunk from the stench that it was giving off.

I sat quiet for a while as he chowed down on the nuts, thinking it must be difficult to chew nuts with only a handful of teeth, but somehow he managed just fine. I looked closely at the map and easily found Maple Lake, its size was vast and covered a huge chunk of Maple Falls itself. It was if Maple Lake was a patient in need of medication to bring it to life and it was those two tributaries that injected life into Maple Lake like morphine seeping through tubes through a catheter into the patient. I followed the snaking rivers with a cold finger that was wrapped in a glove that was struggling to do its job. The map was intriguing, the life being injected into the lake wasn't life at all, but ice.

"There ain't never any Blackfoot sightings until Old Syrup freezes over." Said Chuck matter of factly.

I smiled at him and thought that we may actually get to see whatever this Blackfoot creature was but something in his eyes caused my smile to retreat. His next statement sent a peculiar chilling sensation trickling down my already numb spine.

"That's when the strange shit goes on. You know the disappearances and such!" He stared at me again with those wide eyes, he couldn't conceal the fear. "Of course you know all about those though don't ya? Sure they told you all about the goings on up here in the winter time?" He raised his eyebrows when he was met by stone cold silence and a pale demeanour.

"Guess not." He grunted.

What had I let myself in for?

We reached the town of Maple Falls and as Chuck stopped off for gas I scuttled over to a store to get some supplies. It was a peaceful looking town, quaint. The type of place you'd look at in a book and say to yourself, "I wish I could live there" it was really homely, really nice. But then I thought to myself about the disappearances and wondered what Chuck had meant by that. The town looked fine to me, but I guess looks can be deceiving. I mean, a bird egg looks like a snakes egg but you wouldn't know what was under the shell would you?

I brought some food, snacks and some bottled water. The young man serving me at the register smiled at me and looked out the window over at Chuck's truck.

"You out with Crazy Chuck?"

I told him that I was.

"Good luck!" he scoffed, shaking his head with a huge grin on his face.

As I headed back towards the truck, Chuck was already in the cab with the engine running, waiting on me, obviously eager to move on. I noticed that everybody was looking at me, I could actually feel their eyes burning into me and warming my cold muscles. Were they or was it my own paranoia? All the time I was thinking I must ask about the disappearances, I must know.

We headed off and I wiped the condensation away from the window to reveal dozens of eyes peering at me, through the misty panes of their shops, saloons and diner.

I couldn't sit on it any longer and I splurged it out unceremoniously that I wished to hear about the disappearances.

Chuck laughed out loud "Ain't no way I can tell you about them all. There's to damn many too mention!" He said and with that, sent another blast of chilled bitterness down my back. He told me that there had been 58 disappearances reported since 1999 in the Maple Falls & Blackfoot area.

"58!" I blurted out in dismay.

"Yep!" he cooly replied as if it was nothing.

"That's almost three people missing every year!" I gasped, shaking my head in disbelief.

"Yep!" He smiled "Crazy isn't it? And that's the ones that have been reported."

I actually felt sick, hot vomit had bubbled it's way up my oesophagus and was fizzing around in my throat looking for an escape route.

I managed to pull myself together and took a swig of ice cold water and asked the question that I wasn't sure I wanted the answer too, but I asked it anyway.

"Why are these people disappearing? Who is taking them?"

"Isn't that obvious, Pro-fessor?" Chuck said turning to face me "Why it's The Blackfoot of course!"

We rode the next few hours towards Maple Woods in silence as I tried to compute the answer I'd been given.

I couldn't believe just how quiet The Maple Woods actually were. It was that sort of eery silence that seems to go hand in hand with the fall of snow, almost haunting. The redwoods stood shivering wearing the thick heavy burden of snow overcoats. Peering into the abyss through an uneven congestion of dark tree trunks I saw nothingness, flashes of white on black and black on white like the scene from some old forgotten movie from the silver screen. I no longer felt the small flakes of snow that scratched at my face, nor the chilling breeze that caused my ears to become numb. All I was feeling at this moment was fear. How quickly my emotions had turned on this expedition and we had yet to really start. Gone was the excitement, now replaced with that fear. Was it down to the ghost stories of the disappearances, or caused by the paranoia from the intrusive eyes of the town folk or maybe it was that this guide was crazy and he was leading me into the middle of nowhere. If I was honest with myself I would say all of these elements were at work.

His chunky glove padded down heavily on my shoulder and startled me from my daze, and then I felt the cold again.

"C'mon, Pro-fessor, we go by foot now. Grab your things out of the truck." Chuck said launching a thick chunk of tobacco and spit into a fresh mound of fallen snow.

It would take another couple of hours on foot to reach our destination, Chuck's cabin in the middle of the woods. Again we hardly spoke, I sensed that Chuck knew that he had rattled me and didn't wish to scare me further so he kept tight lipped as we trudged through knee high snow. All around us the towering trees shrouded us and huddled together as if they were plotting against us. I started to distrust the trees.

There was no mention of The Blackfoot, not since the conversation in the truck where he had confessed to me that that is what he thought was responsible for all those missing people, and I as a rational man, had my doubts about that.

It's just a lot of people to go missing due to an apparent mythical creature. I didn't believe that he had any evidence to corroborate this theory. For all I knew it was he, Mr Charles 'Crazy Chuck' Muchnick that was responsible for all the vanishing acts that had been happening in the vicinity over the years. I paused, stopping my over active imagination for a moment to swallow hard with a damning thought, that I was number 59.

We arrived at his cabin, it was consumed in at least two feet of snow and its dark wood made it hard to see. A passerby would have passed it without knowing it was there. But it was quaint and I could see a slightly rusted and worn chimney flute cone protruding out from the thick snow toupee that sat on top of the cabin. I knew then that that

15

meant warmth and that was all I cared about at that moment in time. I chuckled to myself about the earlier statement that Chuck had made about this not being real winter yet and I thought, 'God help me, I'd die out here!' Chuck looked at me with a confused brow as I laughed "Not going stir crazy on me already are ya, Pro-fessor?"

I assured him that I wasn't and we carried on trudging towards the front door, then he hit me with another curious sentence, "It has been known."

Which left yet another question for my brain to try and analyse.

With the temperature dropping rapidly and more snow beginning to fall, there was no way we would be going anywhere for the rest of the afternoon, nor would I want to be out there after dark. The cabin itself was but a one man dwelling place for sure, the size of a shoebox! But it obviously was enough for Chuck. Everything could be seen by just a panning glance from his bed, his toilet, his kitchenette area and log burning stove, which I could not wait to see glowing in all its warming glory. I had also found the place of origin that the damp musty scent that had attached itself to Chuck's racoon hat was coming from, and it was indeed this cabin. It reeked of mildew and roadkill and in one corner of the room stood several bulging cardboard boxes, the word *Blackfoot Shit* was scrawled on each one in shoddy uneducated capitals. I found this very intriguing. I knew that the boxes didn't actually contain the faeces of The Blackfoot, but I was intrigued nonetheless. But in all honesty with the smell of this place I could be wrong. I had never been so glad to see fire in my whole entire lifetime. The warm glow caressed my chapped face and as I closed my eyes listening to the soothing crackling of the embers, amazingly, all seemed right with the world and gone had the fears I had allowed to consume me earlier. With a large piece of matted fur dropped around me (which Chuck assured me was the hide from a Grizzly that he had shot about eight years ago) and my stomach full to burst from Chuck's baked bean supper, I was satisfied. His culinary skills left a lot to be desired but it was warm and filling and as I wiggled my toes in front of the stove swigging a snow cooled Bobby's Light I was finally at peace.

I must have fallen asleep because I woke up shivering, the stove was almost dead, so I sparked it back to life with a fresh chunk of wood and few pokes of the poker. A quick glance at my watch told me it was 1am. It was then that I noticed that Chuck was still awake, his face pressed up against the window a rifle clutched in his hand.

I asked him what it was and I had no reply, he appeared to be in a trance like state and it wasn't until I stood up did he turn around and look at me with those saucer looking eyes of his and said quietly "It's out there, Pro-fessor. I Heard that son of a bitch shuffling around out there."

He looked scared, petrified in fact. Had he been asleep and had something startled him in the middle of a dream and thought The Blackfoot was out there or had he really seen it? I guess we'll never know.

I was woken early, the battered sofa creaked under my tired carcass as the sound of spoon flicking of the sides of a ceramic mug rang in my ears. Through slanted sleepy eyes I looked up at the approaching gummy smile of Chuck, a mug wrapped in a maple leaf, stained with stray drips of a thousand coffees before, the words 'Canada Eh' in black font standing out through the discolouration of the never washed mug.

"Got some bad news for ya, Pro-fessor." Chuck sighed as I sipped my surprisingly good black coffee.

"What's wrong?" I asked him.

"We ain't gonna be going anywhere today. Weather is as fucked up as a soup sandwich out there."

A snow storm had battered us in the earlier hours and it was unwise to venture out in such harshness. But Chuck did make me laugh as he clanked his chipped mug against mine and crowed "Now this is winter!"

The day was not wasted and it was only now that I realised the knowledge on the subject that Chuck was keeping hidden away from everyone under that smelly Raccoon. He told me about how he had been fascinated by the Sasquatch ever since he was a small child. He even went on to say that he saw one on a family picnic trip to Blackleaf when he was just eight years old.

"The image of that hairy fucker just shuffling through the woods without a care in the world, has stayed with me to this day. And probably where my fascination came from I guess." He smiled, you could see he was reminiscing, looking deep into his memory banks for that particular pleasant recollection, then he looked sad. "Folks didn't believe me of course. Got one hell of a whippin' for that I can tell ya!"

"Sorry to hear that." I said, but he just scoffed and smiled that unmistakable grin again and said, "Ah, it's nothing. Pa's belt and I were old friends by then."

He went on to explain that there isn't just one Sasquatch in particular, there are several, subspecies I guess you would call them.

From the first sighting way back in 1811 by David Thompson, who discovered a footprint in the snow at around 14" in length and 8" wide, with just four toes topping it. This took place in Jasper, Alberta.

"Well, Thompson was the first white man to see one anyway. Those redskins used to always be talking about them. That's where the Sasquatch name come from, it's an Indian word, meaning 'Hairy Giant'."

He showed me paper cuttings from all over the globe of sightings of the creature, pages that he had torn from library books with depictions of what they supposedly look like. All the information you could get on them, he had it.

"Folks around here call me crazy. Think I'm a few sandwiches short of a picnic. But take a look at all these sightings! It ain't just me fella. It ain't just me. It goes all around the world! From America to Asia! Even the ruskies got'em too! So how can something that ain't real be seen by so many folk in so many different parts of the world?"

I didn't have an answer for him.

He went on to tell me all the other terms that they were known by. (I have made a list below)

Sasquatch (Hairy Giant)

Bigfoot

Yeti

The Abdominal Snowman

Swampsquatch

Man-Ape

Swamp Ape

With the weather cleared and the snow no longer falling we set off to Old Syrup.

"How far is it to the lake?" I asked Chuck as we'd been trudging through that thigh high snow for around an hour.

"Not long now. About an hour or so."

I sighed, already weary from the expedition and lack of sleep. Chuck laughed at my petulant sighing, his booming laughter echoed through the trees, reverberating of unforgiving redwoods like a frantic pinball machine, it felt like it was the Maple Woods itself that was mocking me.

We passed several cabins and obviously I had questions. It was there that we sat for a break, where I tucked in to a Red Alert energy bar (energy was much needed about now). We slouched on a hollowed out log and I looked at the cabins, they had all been newly renovated and restored and were dotted around in various places within the area like a little community. I made an untimely joke about it maybe being a Yeti village, Chuck didn't see the humour in this. Chuck then went on to tell me yet another bizarre story, starting the conversation with the sentence "I've got a story about this place that'll turn your shit white!"

He told me that the area was originally used for lumberjacks and their families, there was half a dozen cabins or so and a dirt road cut in the wood that follows the Tear Drop River into town, but obviously the road was covered in a couple of feet of snow now and you wouldn't have been able to make out a road even existed.

"Now it was the norm around here that when the winter struck they bailed, you know went and stayed with family and stuff until the worst was over." He said, then he fixated on one cabin in particular and there was the longest pause. He pointed to the cabin nearest us as crumbs fell from my mouth and started to attach themselves to my now heavily stubbled chin.

"Years ago now... God it must be about 20 years back now, a family decided to see the winter through, The Tooth Family. Beau, yeah, Beau Tooth was his name. Well, he was a little behind with his work and he was going to be staying to make up his quota so he had persuaded his wife and two kiddies to stay with him. Thought it would be fun I guess, all that snow for the little ones to play in."

Chuck fell silent again and shook his head, the way that you would when remembering a painful memory that you still can't believe happened. "Well, he went stir crazy did Beau, and he, well, he erm..."

I was hanging on every word, I wanted so badly to know what had happened. Chuck was such a great storyteller that every time he opened that toothless maw of his I was expectant of another gripping yarn.

I was not disappointed.

"That Beau, I mean he was a bear of a man, stood at least 6 feet 8 or 9... Heck he may have even been 7 feet! Large rotund man, built heavily set from lugging all those logs around all day I guess. Well, one night he took his axe and hacked up his wife and two sweet little girls until they were pulp."

I sat gobsmacked, chewed up oats and jam fell from my mouth onto the snow that sat at my feet.

After five minutes of joining him in shaking heads from side to side in disbelief I asked what had happened to him, thinking that maybe he had taken his own life, which is sometimes the case after someone does such a heinous act, the guilt being too much for them to take afterwards. His answer was again a chilling one.

"Don't know." He turned to look at me with those wide eyes, filled with sincerity, this was no ghost story you could see the truth in his eyes. "Nobody knows. He just disappeared."

There was silence again as I stared at the cabin, thinking all the time that he could still be in there. Chuck broke the silence as he rose, wiping snow from the rear of his thick waterproof trousers "If you ask me The Blackfoot got him, only explanation." He said starting to walk away, and not wanting to be left behind, especially not here, I quickly gave chase.

"The cabins are used for tourists now or for hunters during hunting season. But we shouldn't see anyone around this time of year. Hunting season ended last week, so anyone out hunting now could receive a hefting fine if they're caught. Even some jail time."

We reached The Maple Lake (or 'Old Syrup'). It was a beautiful sight to behold, the water so crystal clear it mirrored the shards of dark tree tops and the salmon tinted sky that domed us, that kind of off pinkish tone that seems to appear when there is snow on the way.

"There's been at least six folk disappear from this area alone." Chuck said, standing near the waters edge and pointing in various places. I asked him how he knew.

"There's always shit left behind. Old Blackfoot ain't got no need for rucksacks and such. I've found all sorts, stuff even the authorities miss. You know... hats, wallets, sleeping bags, tents, you know that sort of stuff and even rifles and crossbows from time to time!" Then he turned and looked into my eyes "Even found an arm once."

My face must have been a picture because he smiled.

"A severed arm, must have been pulled clean out of its socket! Just laying there in the thawing snow like it belonged."

I found it very difficult to reply to that, so I didn't even try.

He pointed out that there were several small wooden huts situated around the bank, they resembled old outdoor latrines, only thing missing was the crescent moon cut into the doors.

"Those were put up a few years back now for the fishermen. So they can still fish and not have to worry about the elements."

We trudged over to a wooden dock, layered in thick snow, a bulbous lump protruded from it and I wondered what it could be. Chuck dusted off the layer of snow to reveal a small two man kayak lying turned over on the dock "Have to turn it over, don't want the bastard filling with snow."

He pointed out the Tear Drop Creek that could be seen meeting the lake and it was evidently starting to freeze. "Old Syrup will be frozen over in the next two days."

We settled into the kayak and started to row in unison, this was a little tricky for me to get the hang of, what with being a land lover and all, but Chuck was patient with me and helped me through it and once I got the rhythm it was a lot easier. It was then I could relax and take in the surroundings that are so beautiful and captivating. I even saw some deer, a mother and her tiny fawn shivering in the snow as they drank the ice cold water from the lake. It was a truly magnificent experience that will stay with me forever. The chilling sentence that followed from Chuck would also stay with me as our paddles caressed the still waters "Can't imagine just how many dead bodies and carcasses are floating around underneath us right now."

Thanks for that Chuck, I thought to myself, trying not to look into the water incase I saw the eyes of the dead looking back at me.

"I can only presume that's where Old Blackfoot dumps the bodies. I mean Sasquatch ain't thought of as being carnivorous, but that's what makes Blackfoot different. He's a meat eater alright! But I doubt he'd eat a whole human being hence why he'd throw the left overs in Old syrup here."

My attentions turned to the small island in the centre of the lake, dark and uninviting due to its mass of heavy foliage.

"That's Fisherman's Island. It used to be known to the Indian's as 'Black Death Island'! That's where they believe the Blackfoot originated from. They believe that with its birth it brought with it death and destruction, fire and brimstone type of shit. That's why that patch of woods over yonder..." He pointed over to the left where the trees appeared black and lifeless "...is known as Black Leaf. There was a huge fire there and nothing much grows there now."

It was fascinating to hear about the origins of the places I was seeing and how places were named after the beliefs and superstitions of the Native Americans.

"The island used to be used heavily in the summers originally for fisherman, hence the name, and then more recently by the local teenagers."

"Whatever for?" I asked naively.

"Fucking more than likely! Drinking, smoking, all kinds of shenanigans I imagine. But then when a few of those kids went missing back in '06 nobody tends to go there now."

"Could it be the dwelling place of the Blackfoot do you think?"

"Already checked it way back in '98 or was it '97? Anyway, it's when I started to take the search for the beast seriously and there was nothing there. Haven't been back there since, never really thought there was any point. Maybe I will. Maybe we can check it out on the way back?"

We reached the shore and Blackfoot country in good time, and we tied up the kayak safely for our return, which Chuck said would depending on the condition of the lake, we may be walking back.

"Old Syrup will freeze up solid and we will be able to walk back over it no problem at all. I figure that's how The Blackfoot makes it down to Maple Falls."

I was numb to my surroundings now and each redwood looked like the last or those I had seen in Maple Wood, I found myself probing Chuck for information.

"Do you actually have any hard evidence of The Blackfoot?"

Chuck was a few yards in front of me as we tracked on through the snow and his body language changed, his shoulders slumped forward and his head seemed to drop. I saw an emittance of breath escape as he sighed.

"You don't believe me either, do ya?" He asked.

I reassured him that I did and I was just curious because of the report I was putting together, people will want hard facts. That seemed to win him over and he told me "I guess I've only really got my eyes. I know what I've seen and my eyes don't lie to me Professor. It ain't just seeing shapes and shadows in the woods, I've seen it! Goddamn it have I seen it. Those dark fucking eyes... You see those and they'll haunt your dreams for a lifetime. But, like you say it's just my word and who's going to believe the words of some crazy old bastard like me?"

He went on to show me a secret stash of things he kept in his rucksack, which contained teeth! They looked like animal teeth or could have been human canines, a clump of thick black hair which could have belonged to a black bear, not native to this particular area, but not totally uncommon. I couldn't fully believe him, not even if I wanted to, but I really did want to. Unfortunately there just wasn't enough evidence to back it up, yet. We reached what was known as Holyground, deep in the heart of Blackfoot and we set up camp. Daylight had started to wane and Chuck decided it would be best to get the tent up as soon as possible. He was jittery and kept his rifle very close to him, his attention flitting to each tiny sound. This did not make me feel at ease. We squeezed into the tiny tent and zipped ourselves into the heavy duty sleeping bags that would keep us from dying of frostbite. Chuck settled and became more relaxed, but still he kept his rifle gripped in his gloved hands.

Chuck told me about Blackfoot, how the Natives named it after the beast thinking that if they worshipped it then it wouldn't hurt them. They paid tribute to it by naming their land after it, from Blackfoot Tail, Blackfoot Route, Blackfoot Ridge, Blackfoot Nape and Blackfoot Hill, it was all now collectively known as The Blackfoot Trail.

He pointed out that just twenty miles out of the woods were larger towns like Kowalski Pass, and Pepperville, but most were just smaller towns and settlements. Our plan was to follow the trail towards Blackfoot Ridge to the place where the last disappearance had taken place. A man out running on the trail was never seen again. All that was found was a running shoe and a broken mp3 player. As I started to drift away into a deep sleep all I remember was the festering smell of Chuck's musty raccoon hat.

Now, please be assured that what happened next is the truth. I was jolted awake in the early hours by what sounded like the roar of some unholy beast that could not have been of this earth. Chuck wasn't there and the flap of the tent whipped back and forth in the cold morning breeze. I called to chuck but there was no answer, I will not lie to you I was terrified. I crawled towards the entrance of the tent and my heart pounded rapidly. I could hear it thumping loudly in my ears but it didn't drown out that horrendous growl when I heard it again. I shivered and shook peering outside. Then I heard Chuck scream, and the rifle went off, deafening me for a few seconds causing me to wince. I stumbled out of the tent and suddenly suffered a vile blow to the head that knocked me silly. I collapsed to the floor into the cold unforgiving snow. Before I could gain my bearings, Chuck came tumbling over the tent and landed in a pile next to me. He sat bolt upright screaming "It's here, it's here!" His face was cut and bloodied, lacerated, like his flesh had been torn with some claw or sharp implement. My vision was blurry, my head was woozy and I was on the verge of falling into an unconscious state. But as I fought the inevitable, I turned to where Chuck's terrified wide eyes were fixated and through the soft fluttering of snowflakes, as God is my witness, I saw it! I saw The Blackfoot! An exceptionally large dark figure disappeared into the woods but before it left, I saw those eyes. At first I thought they were just dark

29

empty sockets but then light glistened on them, glasslike, like two black marbles. The darkest eyes I've ever seen, and as it disappeared and my eyes rolled back into my head, I remember thinking that there was no human being that could have eyes as black as that.

After that I must have blacked out as I don't remember anything apart from waking up in a hospital bed in Downtree, being treated for hypothermia and concussion. Next to me sat a smiling Chuck Muchnick, several stitches embroidered across his face, Racoon hat still sitting on his head without a care in the world and he said but one thing through that toothless smile "I told you it was real."

Now, I have obviously told this story to many people and there are still the sceptics, those that will pick holes in it so that the story fits their way of thinking. I've heard all the theories.

'You were almost unconscious, it could have been anything!'

'It was probably a bear!'

'Muchnick hit you over the head and staged the whole thing.'

'You had become stir crazy, you were seeing things that weren't there.'

I know I have come out of this without any evidence apart from my own experience, but I can say with my hand on my heart that there is something out there, something dark and hideous dwells in that cold wintery abyss and each winter it comes out to feed. It may not be a Blackfoot, A Yeti or Sasquatch it may in fact be much worse than any of those, but there is something there.

Ironically I will finish this report quoting Mr Charles 'Chuck' Muchnick by saying, "I guess I've only really got my eyes. I know what I've seen and my eyes don't lie to me."

Sheriff Patrick Russell shook his head as he took one final drag of his wilting Freebird cigarette, simultaneously blowing out the smoke and vigorously jabbing the cigarette butt into the ashtray, that sits next to him on his woodworm ridden office desk.

His face was lit by the brightness of his laptop screen and magically smoke circled him like a wagon train taking defensive measures against attacking natives. He shook his head again, slamming the lid of his laptop down and forcing the office into a gloomy haze.

"What a load of horse shit!" He scoffed.

CHAPTER 2

The wind howled like the distant baying of a lone wolf greeting a full moon with reverence. The snow flakes were now thick and coated with tiny clusters of icy droplets. Winter had officially arrived in Maple Falls.

The snow fell in a relentless flurry, as though it were the contents of a festive snow globe, covering all that lay beneath with its numbing shroud. A large stag materialised from the cover of dominating redwoods and snow lathered foliage. Cautiously it looked around, surveying the area, making sure it was safe to move forward into the small clearing that still had some green shrubbery rising from the pure white canvas. Its black eyes suspicious of the quiescent setting, its dark nostrils that were damp from the cold twitched, the scent of something foreign to it lingered in the air. Its large ears fluttered, manoeuvring themselves like aerials trying to attain a signal, but there was nothing. There was no sound in The Maple Woods tonight, nothingness, as the silent onslaught of Mother Nature's wintery veil continued to fall. Surprisingly dainty on its hooves for such a large muscular creature, it trod through the picturesque layer of undisturbed snow, leaving circular hoof marks in its tentative strides. It reached the shrub, the urge to devour it in one bite nagging at its conscious, but the majestic beast was true to its instincts and remained watchful of its surroundings. A flick of the ears and another twitch of the nostrils and it had finally decided it was safe to commence. It began to eat, tearing at the cold greenish stem and leaves, chewing vigorously in obvious satisfaction.

Elroy Pascoe sat safely nestled between a fallen log and surrounded by snow covered shrubs. He was dressed head to toe in white and grey camouflage, a winter soldier if ever there was one, with his gas-operated semi-automatic rifle gripped in his gloveless hands. He'd removed his gloves when he had first seen the stag move through the trees ahead and sat in wait, with his rifle poised and aimed ready. His fingers were cold, incredibly cold, left hand cupping the Turkish walnut forestock while the index finger of his right hand hovered tentatively over the trigger. He waited, left eye closed tightly, right eye socket pressed firmly against the sight of the scope, the stag now settled in between its crosshairs. And still he waited, this was by no means his first rodeo and he wasn't going to make the mistake of getting too excited and pulling that trigger until precisely the right moment.

The awkward position he had taken up had started to take its toll on his legs that were already cold and weary from the hike through the snow from Maple Cross. They had now begun to seize up so he was going to have to pull the trigger soon before his middle aged carcass toppled over.

He adjusted his positioning slightly and that caused the snow below to crunch, the stag's head immediately rose from its meal and inspected the woods, black eyes looking in Elroy's direction. The stag froze as did Elroy, sweat now amazingly seeping from under his thick woollen hat and down his heavily stubbled face.

"Stay right where you are, you fucker." Elroy whispered

"Don't you be running off no place, you hear me?"

The deer's satellite dish ears twirled around again, its dark eyes not daring to blink. After a few minutes of this, finally the deer lowered its head and began to eat again. Elroy could wait no longer and pulled down hard on the cold metal trigger, the bullet hurtled through the barrel and tore through the gullet of the young stag, which then fell unceremoniously into a heap in the snow. The sound of the gunshot was still ringing in the air as Elroy's joints cracked and he staggered to his feet, trying to get some life back into his strained muscles.

"Gotcha! You little bastard!" He laughed at the top of his voice, the sound of his laughter joining the echoing gunshot in a short peculiar symphony.

He trudged through the knee high snow. With the easy part done, now came the hard part of getting 200 pounds worth of dead weight back to his truck which was situated in Maple Cross a few miles away.

The moist black eye of the stag looked up at Elroy, a lifeless glare that seemed to say, 'How could you?' Elroy caught his grinning reflection in the eye and prodded the carcass with the business end of his rifle.

It was dead all right.

Blood seeped from its throat, its heat melting the snow that lay beneath, the warm steam rising in the cold evening air.

"Got you in the end. Old Elroy Pascoe never misses boy." He boasted.

He grabbed the stag's long protruding antlers and gave them a shake.

"Got me a nice new decoration for the den" He gloated.

Somewhere in the abyss a branch snapped, and this time it was Elroy Pascoe's eyes that were wide and wary. He grabbed his rifle in both hands and looked all around, his ears weren't as finely tuned as the stags, so it was impossible for him to pinpoint just where the sound came from.

"Anybody there?" He called out into the woods, hearing only his own echo in multiple fading replies. He looked jittery as he turned on the spot feeling like he was now the prey. He had every right to be jittery, hunting season had closed three weeks ago and if he was caught, he could be fined a considerable amount as well as the possibility of doing some jail time.

Elroy Pascoe could ill afford either of those things to happen.

He finally calmed down "Probably just a coon!" He sniffed and turned his attention back to his catch, which was now empty of its warm plasma.

"Best get you back to the cabins and move you properly in the morn."

There was another snap in the woods, louder this time and closer.

"What the fuck!" Elroy blasted, almost jumping out of his boots.

He grabbed the gun even tighter now and fear worked its way down his throat with a gulp "Who the fuck's there?" He called again his echo stuttering, exposing the fear that lay within.

"Whoever's out there better back off! I ain't to be fucked with, D'you hear?" The words carried for miles as he stood shivering.

"You hear me?" He shouted even louder. There was nothing, no reply and when the echo died again there was silence. He took off his woollen hat and wiped his sweat covered receding brow with it, before stuffing it into the pocket of his thick Parker.

"Time to get the hell out of this fucking place." He said to himself as he turned his attentions back again to the stag, sliding his rifle strap over his torso so that his hands were now free.

"Maybe Crazy Chuck was right. Maybe these woods are haunted." He murmured to himself, but not really believing what he was saying.

Crack went another branch too close for comfort this time and he span around ready to give a mouthful to whoever was fucking with him. But nothing came from his mouth, not a whisper of air left his now gaping and quivering maw. His eyes wide with horror, amazingly his face looked childlike as a dark towering shadow swept across and consumed him. He didn't even struggle, it was though he was rooted to the spot like a small withering tree.

He saw the axe rise into the air and helplessly his dewy eyes stared at it, his life flashing dismally before him. Snowflakes clung to the axe as it waited, hovering in the air for the right moment to strike. Suddenly there was the singing sound of it cutting through the air and the horrific crunching of bone as the axe's bit wedged itself into his face and skull. The body of Elroy Pascoe fell into a heap next to the stag's carcass and the sound of heavy congested breathing now echoed around the woods. The axe was removed with an aggressive yank, sending blood splattering onto the white snow, blotching it like a Rorschach inkblot test.

Gently snowflakes fell into the carved out canyon of Elroy Pascoe's now featureless face and once again there was silence in the woods of Maple Falls.

CHAPTER 3

Sheriff Patrick Russell had said his goodbyes to his wife Holly, and started his short journey to work in his Sheriff department issue 4x4, lathered in Canadian red and white and plastered with Sheriff decals. It was a very reliable Ford F150 Lariat with its hefty tyres safely ploughing through the few inches of snow that had fallen in the night and lay untraversed.

Sheriff Russell moved cautiously and slowly, he'd get to the office when he got there, there was no need to rush, not in this weather. *That's how accidents happen* he thought to himself.

He turned on the radio and he cringed as his ears were met with a very loud *Like a Virgin,* buzzing through the speakers. His thick mousy horseshoe moustache contorted and he let out a groan as he immediately lowered the volume to a respectable level, he then fiddled with the radio knob tuning the dial to Radio Blackfoot on the 190.4 frequency.

"Goddamn it, Raymond!" He cursed, as he vigorously retuned the radio.

The radio was also at sixes and sevens when Deputy Clegg had borrowed his truck, always favouring the sounds of the eighties at 120.18 (The 80's Fire station) over Sheriff Russell's country music preference.

With the sultry tones of *Shania Twain* now appeasing his mood, he relaxed back into the driver's seat and let the warmth from the heater bathe his middle aged, rugged but handsome face.

"At least it's stopped snowing." He said gazing through the windshield as the truck rolled out of Maple Drive and into Maple Falls itself.

He waved to shopkeepers busy opening up their little stores for another days business. He'd only been in Maple Falls for six months, but he was made to feel so welcome by everyone there. He saw the job as a step up the ladder as his former position was Deputy at a small town called Crimson. Although originally the position was meant to be temporary as the last Sheriff (Sheriff Windwood) had gone absent without leave, but obviously he was expected back.

He never came back.

Obviously this was a strange situation, but listening to the locals of Maple Falls, Keith Windwood had become a little senile in his ageing years and many say he was no longer capable of doing the job.

He hadn't gotten more than halfway through the main high street when his car radio let out a loud cackle, annoyance slapping the face of Sheriff Russell as he was enjoying the last few moments of the song.

"Sheriff, C'mon in, Sheriff, over?" Came the crackled voice of Lieutenant Adams on the other end.

"Go ahead, Tammy." He sighed.

I haven't even gotten into the office yet and already they're hassling me! He thought bitterly.

"Sorry to bother you, Sheriff, I know it's early." Tammy said softly and apologetic.

Immediately he felt bad and took it back.

It comes with the territory, Patrick. You want the pay-check, you gotta be available 24/7.

"Go ahead, Tammy."

"We've received a frantic phone call from Marlena Pascoe. Seems old Elroy hasn't returned home from his weekend's erm..."

"Hunting?" He said shaking his head, knowing that hunting season had finished now and if he had been hunting, this meant more bullshit and paperwork for him to deal with.

"Erm... Yes, Sheriff."

"Fine, I'll pay her a visit when I've touched base. Got a few files to sort out before I do anything else."

"Okay, Sheriff."

He was about to end the call and continue his crawl to the office when Tammy spoke again.

"Oh, Sheriff?"

"Yeah, Tammy?"

"Raymond wanted me to remind you that it's your turn to get the bagels this morning." Faint laughter could be heard in the background, It was Deputy Clegg.

"Tell Deputy Clegg, he can suck my dick!" He shouts down the receiver.

Laughter erupts from the radio, several different tones and pitches of laughter can be heard.

"As if I've got fucking time to be fetching breakfast for that ass-hat!" Then he smiled imagining a group of officers all gathered around the radio having a good laugh.

"I'll tell him. Over and out!" came the calm response from lieutenant Adams.

He shook his head and chuckled to himself, he did enjoy the ribbing, it was part of the game, plus his crew were a good bunch and he liked to keep things friendly.

No, it wasn't a bad town overall and it's not as though he was rushed off his feet really, just tedious paperwork which comes with all professions these days. It could be worse, there could be rapes and murders to deal with on a daily basis, thankfully nothing like that goes on here. The occasional domestic dispute or theft, or drunken shenanigans at *Chopper's* bar. No nothing major, apart from the strange amount of disappearances in these parts there's nothing to write home about. Besides he put these so called 'disappearances' down to people just getting fed up with the monotony of small town living and moving on.

He sighed again wondering if he would ever get to work this morning as he pulled over to the side of the road directly adjacent to *Dawn's,* the best diner in Maple Falls, the only diner in Maple Falls.

He got out of the Lariat slamming the door behind him and his face was hit by that cold unforgiving Canadian wind, he shuddered and wrapped his unzipped moss coloured Parker around his freshly pressed uniformed torso and headed inside.

The diner was full, as it was most mornings. The majority of locals would come out to enjoy one of Dawn's breakfasts and a gossip over coffee. Dawn knew everything that was going on in town, sometimes even more than Sheriff Russell himself, he would playfully call her his intel.

"Good morning, Sheriff!" Dawn called from behind the counter, while juggling a hot steaming coffee pot and a plate of scrambled eggs on a bed of french toast.

"How's it going, Dawn?" He asked casually leaning on the counter and gesturing good morning to the locals with waves and nods.

"Oh you know, same old shit!" She cackled, her voluptuous bosom bouncing up and down on her bulbous belly as she served.

"You need to get some help in here, I've told you before." He smiled, comfortably leaning his hand on the handle of his issue Glock 17.

"And I've told you Sheriff, ain't nobody gonna work for peanuts, and I pay peanuts!" They both laughed "Now I've got lots to do today Sheriff, ain't no time for standing around warbling. I've got these ruffians to feed as well as a party arriving to fill one of the cabins."

"Oh really? What party is that?" The Sheriff questioned. Again Dawn proved she knew more or less what was going on around here than he did.

"A party of youngsters, students. They're renting out one of my cabins for a week."

"Strange time of year for anyone to be coming up here don't ya think?"

"Yeah, probably. Apparently they're here to study, but who knows with these kids today what they're going to get up to."

"Do you think it's wise renting it out to them then?"

"Sheriff, I need the money! These bagels don't buy themselves." She smiled handing him a paper bag filled with bagels that she had already prepared for him.

"I guess you're right." He smiles back at her and takes the

41

bag, handing over a $20 dollar bill in exchange. It was too much of course but he always overpaid her, she worked damn hard here all on her own, as well as keeping those two cabins she owned in immaculate condition whatever time of year, he figured she earned the tip.

"This is too much Sheriff!"

But he was already leaving "I'll see you around Dawn."

"Thanks Sheriff!" She smiled at him, a warm motherly smile. He opened the door and stopped for a moment, pondering. "Oh, Dawn?" He asked.

"Yes, Sheriff?"

"I'll keep and eye on those kids for ya. You know just in case."

"Thank you Sheriff. That's mighty good of you!"

"What time are they collecting the keys?"

"Around lunch time, maybe a little later. Depends if they get lost or not. You know how easy it is to get turned around in Maple."

"Indeed I do."

CHAPTER 4

"Erm...I think we're lost, you guys!" Jessica reluctantly leaks out through gritted teeth, as she takes the sleeve of her coat and wipes away the layer of condensation that had smothered the passenger side window, revealing row upon row of snow covered redwoods.

"It's gotta be around here someplace!" Quack moaned as he peered through the windshield, his large rotund stomach the consistency of jello as it pressed up against the steering wheel. "I can't see shit out here, it all looks the same!"
This was much to the displeasure of some of the other passengers, who sat in the rear of the vintage 1983 Vandura cargo van. Well, one of them.

"Oh for fuck's sake!" Groaned Rob from the backseat in annoyance, "How the hell did that fat fuck get us lost on a straight road?"

"Hey Jock strap! I heard that!" Quack fired back.

"Well, I said it loud enough for you to hear you fat fuck!" Rob growled.

"Oh, that's original!" mocked Quack "It's fucking glandular you dipshit!"

"It's fucking burgers!" Laughed Rob.

Mia had been sat in silence for the last 10 miles, patiently working her way through Chapter 15 of *Hartwaker: The Realm of Maglore* and was so annoyed to be disrupted that she yelled at the top of her lungs "Will you assholes give it a rest!" There was now total silence as the other six folks turned to stare at her. But it did the trick and the bickering ceased. Now satisfied, she went back to her book.

Sophie sat in between bookworm Mia and grumpy jock Rob, she'd been going steady with him for a few months now. Captain of the chess club and the star quarterback in a relationship meant that the saying is true, opposites do attract.

"Will you just calm down, Rob!" Sophie whispered holding his large muscular bicep with her dainty fingers.

"I don't know why you dragged me along anyway! I've got nothing in common with these gee..." He looked at her, a disapproving look staring back at him over circular lensed glasses "... These... people!"

Sophie smiled and stroked his arm affectionately "These are my friends, Rob."

"I know! But that Quack guy just rubs me up the wrong way!"

"Please just try, for me?" She smiles again and he smiles back.

"Sure" He shrugs and they kiss, the pecks of lips become more passionate and they are soon making out on the backseat. Mia oblivious now as she has settled down into her fantasy world once more.

Dustin and Max who are sat in the centre of the van on swivelling chairs, currently in the middle of a legendary game of Pro Champion Trumps, avert their eyes and watch as Rob's large hand manoeuvres its way up Sophie's soft lemon cotton blouse, pawing lustfully at her pert breast. The pair stare at the frolicking teens with eyes wide and mouths wider, the shape of her breast bulging out from underneath its confines and that is enough to make Dustin and Max sweat.

Hypnotised by such a pastime that they are unacquainted with, they begin to unknowingly drop their wrestling trump cards onto the worn carpeted floor of the van. Gone is Dustin's winning hand of The Slammer, Randy Rogan and Johnny Midnight, Max's Firecrackers and Megan Powers join them as drool has started to drip from Dustin's dark bulging bottom lip and Max frequently closes his eyes and then opens them again to see if what they are witnessing is real.

"Hey, you pair of Perverts!" Cries Mia disapprovingly.

They're both immediately snapped from their depraved gawking.

"Give it a rest will ya?" Mia says shaking her head at them before focusing on her book again.

"We weren't doing anything!" Says Max groping at his sweatshirt trying to pull it down over a suspicious growth that had formed in his jeans, dropping the rest of his cards in the process, there goes Emily Kincaid, Yellow Feather and Jungle Jim. The commotion is enough to stop Sophie and Rob from rounding second base (Not that Sophie would, especially not here, but Rob didn't know that).

"Were you guys watching us?" Sophie asked, adjusting her blouse.

45

Max shook his head frantically as Dustin scratched nervously at his short afro, smiling awkwardly.

"Sorry Soph!" Dustin scoffed.

"Eww! You guys are gross!"

She adjusted her seating and wrapped her open coat around herself.

"Shit, you guys! Talk about cock blocking!" Rob sneered at them, visually terrifying the two who hit the deck of the van to retrieve their cards like nothing had happened.

"Cock blocking?" Sophie said turning to him "You think we were going to... I mean... in here? Now?"

"Soph I..." Rob tries, but is cut off by Sophie turning away from him. The two sat in silence both of them sulking, arms folded in mirroring petulance.

Rob mouthing the words "You're dead!" To Max and Dustin who ever so slowly turned on the swivel chairs to face the front of the van.

"He's gonna kill us, Maximus." Dustin whispered.

"Yep!" Maximus whispered back "But, did you see her tit?"

The pair made eye contact and began to snigger uncontrollably.

Jessica shakes her head smiling at the antics going on behind her and turned her attention back to the road map on her lap.

"So any ideas, Quack?" Jessica asked.

"We must have missed a turning somewhere. If I continue down this road it's going to take us to Talon!"

Jessica gazed at the map again, enjoying the warmth spluttering out of the heater, it was nice and comforting, in fact the van might have been a steaming pile of junk, but there was nothing wrong with the heating, it was almost tropical in there.

They were in for a rude awakening when they left its warming bosom and into the raw glacial chill outside, that will stab at them like a thousand sharp icicles, hitting their entire body in one fell swoop.

"Maybe if I try my cell again?" Jessica said, retrieving her cell phone from her jacket pocket.

"Good idea!" Said Quack "I'll pull over and see if we can get our bearings."

Jessica tapped away at the large touch screen as Quack pulled it up to the side of the road, hazard lights switched on to indicate their whereabouts to any other vehicles on the road. Not that there were any other vehicles on the road, in fact they had hardly seen any other cars since leaving Crimson.

"Yes!" Jessica cried "I finally have some signal."

"Right on!" Quack smiled, his round face caked in sweat from trying to control this rickety beast through such treacherous conditions. He dabbed at his brow with a rag that he used to wipe the windows with.

"What's going on?" Came the irritable caterwauling from Rob.

"Nothing!" Quack snapped "Just all sit tight for a minute."

"Shit, we're lost aren't we?" Max gulped "I don't want to get raped by any toothless local out here!"

"What toothless locals have you seen out here?" Dustin scoffed "There's nobody out here!"

"Yeah, well you hear stories." Max adds looking around cautiously.

"You've got more chance of being eaten by a Yeti around these parts!" Laughed Sophie.

"Yeti's!" Max and Dustin gulped, playfully embracing each

other and shaking.

"Yeah, one of you dipshits might get dragged off into the woods and get drilled by one of them!" Rob chortled to himself "Only chance you two have of getting laid."

"Damn!" Dustin cringed "Imagine being dry humped by a Yeti!"

They both simulated vomiting noises.

"It's actually The Blackfoot." Mia said, not even looking up from her book.

"A what now?" Sophie asked.

"Blackfoot. That's what the Sasquatch are referred to around these parts."

"Blackfoot?" Dustin laughed "Hey! I've got a black foot!" And with that bent Max over the swivel chair and simulated buggery with the toe of his right hiking boot probing Max's rectum. The swivel chair was obviously not made to withstand such antics and it span around quickly causing them to fall to the floor in hysterics. The laughter was contagious and soon all the passengers in the rear were joining in wholeheartedly.

"Got it!" Jessica squealed delightedly with glee.

"You found it?" Quack said.

"Sure have!" She smirked.

"How far have I got to go back?" Sighed Quack, already preparing himself for a lengthy drive back from where they came.

"You haven't. There's a turning to Maple Falls about a mile down the road."

"You're kidding me?" Quack said, shaking his head.

Max wipes away the condensation from his window and looks out into the mass of trees. He squints tightly trying to focus into the dense woodland, wondering what secrets it conceals. With his nose pressed against the cold glass and his warm breath starting to fog it up once again he asked a question, to nobody in particular, maybe it was only meant for his ears, but it was solemn when he asked "What if there really is something out there?"

Suddenly a gargantuan snow plough truck erupted, a sound like thunder that knocked Max backwards off his seat in fright, the others bursting into fits of uncontrollable terrified screams. The van is rocked back and forth as it is bombarded by a mass of snow.

The screaming stopped and there were sniggers as they realised it was just a passing snowplough, its rear red glowing lights disappearing into the mist ahead. As they came to their senses the van continued to sway, its weary chassis creaking as if it had had enough and longed to be parked up somewhere warm out of this damned cold.

Sure enough a mile or so down the road they were met by a large sign 'WELCOME TO MAPLE FALLS, THE HOME OF THE LUMBERJACK'

The van erupts with euphoric cheers and when they had all read the sign they all called out "Lumberjack!"

They turn onto Maple Drive with their own rendition of... 'I'm a Lumberjack and I don't care, I sleep all night and I work all day...' as they disappear into a congregation of scheming redwoods, their pine covered branches intertwining together to contrive the eerie gloom.

CHAPTER 5

It was 4pm by the time Sheriff Russell looked up from his mass of paperwork he'd completed. He emitted a fatigued sigh, one that said, 'What the hell am I doing here? I'm so bored and nothing ever happens here'.

He brushed the thought aside and counted his blessings. He lent back in his creaky office chair and rubbed at his eyes, sighing again. He grabbed the handle of his mug and tilted it towards him, it was empty, realising now that he finished his last black coffee about two hours ago now and thought to himself that another one was probably in order. He leaned forward and placed his mug back down on the desk, fitting almost perfectly back into the rings of a thousand coffees past and sighed again. He could not get around it, he was bored, he wanted some action. He looked at the pile of files that had taken a lot longer than expected to accomplish, but he was satisfied nonetheless.

He surveyed his office, well, it was still technically Sheriff Windwood's office, even had his certificates and photographs on the wall. Plus the one thing that annoyed him the most, Windwood's name was still stencilled on the frosted glass for all to see. Maybe this was why he didn't feel at home, because it was like wearing somebody else's underwear. I guess he'd never truly feel settled until they heard from Windwood.

He stared at a photograph of Sheriff Keith W. Windwood, dressed smartly in his uniform as he stood shaking hands with the withered looking Mayor Thorn, who was the elected official from the neighbouring town, Crimson.

"Hey Keith! Did you ever get this much damn paperwork?" There was a knock at the door, and he swivelled on his chair to face it, the creaky melody acting as background music to his gruff vocals "Come in!"

"Afternoon, Sheriff!" came the pleasant greeting from Lieutenant Tammy Adams.

Even the cheerful greeting couldn't stop the groan from climbing up his throat and bursting out of his mouth as he saw another stack of files pressed tightly to her bosom. "Got some more paperwork for ya." She sniggered.

"Will it never end?" He said, throwing his arms into the air and collapsing onto the desk.

"It's all go in Maple Falls, isn't it Sheriff?" she smiled, placing them on his desk.

"Tammy, how can a town where literally nothing happens, conjure up so much goddamn paperwork?" He asked in all seriousness.

Tammy grabbed the first file from the pile and dropped it into his lap "That's for the theft of Drew Cartwright's tractor." Then the next bulging file "The court summons for old Mr Ygoravic, who refused to pay his rent to Dawn." The file after that slapped down into the ever increasing mountain of paperwork on his lap "That one is about that bizarre business with Crazy Chuck and Professor Cumberbatch from last year!"

She reached for the next one, but he stopped her with a gentle grab of her hand and then patted it.

"Okay, I get the picture, Tammy." He smiled.

She smiled a motherly smile at him, the kind that tells you everything will be all right. "You'll get the hang of it, Sheriff."

She was about ten years his senior, but she acted older, like a mother hen just trying to make everyone feel okay, he guessed she just liked looking after people.

"Thank you, Tammy. I don't know what I'd do without you!" He smiled.

She patted his hand "Anytime, Sheriff." She said, turning to leave but then stopped "You know something? Keith used to say exactly the same thing to me." Then she shrugged "Weird, huh? I wonder where that old buzzard has got too?"

"Yeah, me too!" He sighed, stacking the files into a pile on his desk. He was about to crack his knuckles and attempt to work his way through them when he heard Tammy call from the corridor "Oh, Sheriff?"

"Yeah?" He replied.

"It's after four and you still haven't been to see Marlena Pascoe!"

"Oh, Dog Shit!" He said rising from his chair.

"And you haven't been to check to see if those out-of-towners have arrived yet."

"Fucking, Pig shit!" he yelped reaching for his hat that was hanging on a coat stand, it wobbled under the vigorous yank and he slicked his longish hair back before placing his hat firmly on his head.

"Oh, and you haven't called your wife back." Her voice got quieter each time as she moved further away.

"Oh, double fucking chicken shit!" He growled grabbing his thick Parker and began putting it on as he left his office and then was met by the knockout blow when Lieutenant Adams said, "Oh, and Raymond's taken your truck out."

"Oh..." He screamed, his face blushing before immediately simmering and then sighing whispering to himself "...Shit."

CHAPTER 6

Two hours later than scheduled, Quack's van pulled up slowly next to Dawn Rougeau's diner, cutting through the soft snowy sludge that had been churned up by the daily flow of vehicles through the high street.

"Here we are! Told you I'd get us here in one piece!" announced Quack, brimming with pride.

"Our hero!" Jessica said smiling at him, before pecking at his chubby cheek with a friendly thankful kiss.

"Stop it! You'll make old Quackster blush!"

There was an abundance of buzzing sounds within the van as they all pulled up the zips of their thick warm coats, it sounded like a colony of angry wasps had been disturbed.

"Everybody out!" Called Jessica and she jumped out of the passengers side and quickly moved around to the side door and slid it open, allowing the cold wintery air to infiltrate the van and cause the unsuspecting passengers to shudder, as though someone had just trudged over their graves.

"It's about friggin time you got us here!" Rob scoffed, cutting a sneering glare at Quack, who was looking past him and watching Sophie tie her long blonde hair back in a tail. Every chance Quack got he would stare at Sophie, boy was he enamoured with her.

"You hear me, Duckworth?" Rob reiterated, not wanting his

verbal provoking to go unnoticed.

"Screw you!" Quack sneered, now even more annoyed at Rob.

Rob pushed past Max and Dustin and exited the van.

"Chivalry is dead I see!" scoffed Mia shaking her head and looking at Sophie who sheepishly smiled back at her and came automatically to his defence "Oh, I'm sure he didn't mean it, Mia."

Mia tutted and exited the van too.

Max and Dustin allowed Sophie to go first, both of them bowing down in unison, crowing 'M'lady' in an awful English accent.

"Thank you kind Sirs." Sophie giggled as she attempted to climb out.

"Do you need any help stepping down, Soph?" Quack asked sweetly, still hauled up in the driver's seat, wedged snuggly under the steering wheel.

"No thanks, Quack. I think I got this." She replied smiling at him, a smile that melted his heart and warmed his loins.

"Well, you be careful, there may be some black ice under that snow." He added.

Max and Dustin then spent several minutes playfully bowing to each other saying, "After you, Sire!" "No, no, after you, Sire" and on and on before they collapsed in a fit of laughter, and tumbled out of the van.

Jessica slid the door across and then attempted to shut the door but she gazed over at Quack who was watching Rob and Sophie cuddle and kiss on the sidewalk.

"You okay, Quack?" Jessica asked quietly.

"Huh? Oh, yeah I'm okay. I think I'll stay in the van." His sad face forced a smile at Jessica who nodded and smiled back. It broke her heart to see her friend so sad, she knew what a great guy he was and what he could offer a girl, even if Sophie didn't.

She slammed the door shut and Quack's sad round face continued to watch Sophie through the fogging windows.

"Okay, you guys!" Jessica announced clapping her hands together (and wishing she'd put her gloves on that were warming themselves on the balmy dashboard) "Let's go and get the keys!"

"We're going to the store." Max said smiling and nudging Dustin.

"Oh, yeah! We need some new reading material." Dustin added.

"Okay, don't be long!" Jessica said, rolling her eyes, knowing perfectly well that they're going to try and get the latest copy of the popular adult magazine, *Heyboy.*

"I've heard that Barbie Butkus is the centrefold this month!" Whispered Max as the two scuttled over the road, their sneakers slipping and sliding as they awkwardly went on their way.

Jessica looked over at Rob and Sophie who had slunk into the doorway of an old closed down hardware store, the name on the sign had flaked away from years of weather damage, but the name *Thurman's* could just be made out. The couple began taking part in some heavy petting once again.

"Guess it's just me and you then." She said pleasantly and upbeat and was met by the unenthusiastic response of "Go us!" from Mia.

The pair of them entered Dawn's diner as Quack's bottom lip wobbled vigorously as he watched Rob devour Sophie's face through a wintery frame.

Dawn was busy wiping down tables when the girls entered, *Vanda and the Hell Sings* blared on the old radio that sat on the counter, a thick layer of electrical tape wrapped around its broken antenna. There was only one customer in at the time, an old gentleman that sat up at the bar of the diner on a stool, struggling to open a sachet of sugar in a shaking arthritic grip.

"Well, hello, girls!" Dawn cried, wiping off the table with her cloth and then stuffing it into her apron pocket.

"Hi!" Beamed Jessica, "Are you Mrs Rougeau?"

"Ms, if you don't mind!" Dawn said jokingly "But you can call me Dawn." She said, smiling that warm motherly smile at them as she approached.

"Pleased to meet you. I'm Jessica, this is Mia."
Mia forced out a smile.

"Warm enough for ya?" Dawn laughed.

"It is a little chilly." Jessica laughed "We spoke on the phone? I'm very sorry we're late but we..."

"Got lost? Yeah I know." Dawn smiled.

"Yeah, How'd you know?" Jessica asked.

"Everybody gets lost on their virgin trip to Maple Falls, my dears." Dawn said nonchalantly, as she wandered off towards the counter and whipped the sugar out of the old man's shaking hands.

"Give that here, Sparky!" She sighed and ripped the sachet open and sprinkled the sugar into his steaming coffee.

"Now! I guess you girls have come for the keys?"

"Yes, please!" Replied Jessica.
Dawn slid behind the counter and rummaged around underneath it.

She pulled out the keys and handed them to Jessica, a large wooden maple leaf keyring hung from it with the number 3 etched into it.

"There you go. You've got cabin number 3." Dawn smiled.

"No! Really?" Said Mia sarcastically, rolling her eyes behind her thick rimmed glasses. Dawn was not amused and frowned at Mia.

"I'll let that one slide, missy. I once had that same me versus the world mentality when I was your age!"

"Mia!" Jessica scalded her.

"Ha! It's okay." Dawn waved it away with a chapped red hand "One winter in Maple Falls is enough to beat that out of ya. Believe me!"

"What's the best way to get there?" Jessica asked "The maps online aren't very clear to the cabin's whereabouts."

"It won't be on no map. Or no fancy-pants inter-web contraption neither!" She scoffed, the girls both sniggered, Dawn ignored them and continued "The cabins are cut into The Maple Woods themselves. All you have to do is follow the dirt road that runs along side Tear Drop Creek, it's only about half a mile from here. It's sign posted at the end of the high street. Look for Lumberjack's Cabins on the sign at the crossroads."

"Thank you so much!" Jessica smiled and they turned to leave.

"Just a minute!" Dawn said with seriousness in her voice. They both turned around.

"Look, I know you got some boys with ya, and that's fine. I'm sure your Mama's have brought you up to respect yourselves and your bodies."

"Oh, Brother!" Mia murmured and got a swift elbow in the ribs from Jessica.

"But whatever goes on, I want you to know I won't stand for any drugs! None whatsoever! And if I find the remains of just one joint, I'll be in touch with your parents or guardians. I have your numbers remember."

"Oh, no, Ms Rougeau, there will be nothing like that going on. We are going to use the time to study before the tests we have coming up."

"Say no more about it!" Dawn said drawing a line underneath the conversation and going back to her pleasant smiling self.

"I've made you a flask of coffee to take with you." She said plopping the large flask on the counter "And here is a bag of cupcakes for you all." A brown paper bag was slid right next to the flask and she smiled at them.

"Oh wow, you really didn't need to do that! But thank you so much." Answered Jessica excitedly, as she lifted up the hefty flask and Mia grabbed the bag.

"Now, go and have fun." Dawn added as they walked towards the door.

"We will. Thanks again!" Jessica said.

"Just make sure you guys be safe out there. It is the wilderness you know and there'll be another helping of snow fall tonight, so you need to take care."

"We will!" Jessica smiled.

Dawn returned the smile with a little nod, before remembering something else.

59

"Oh! I've left a list of handy phone numbers on a notepad next to the telephone, if you get into any difficulties."

"Okay, thanks!"

And with that they left.

"Nice girl!" Sparky said stirring his coffee ever so slowly "Didn't like the gook though." He sniffed.

"Jeff Thurman! I will not allow you to talk like that in my diner!" She scalded.

"Now, drink your coffee!" she sighed, watching as they all piled into the van and it drove away.

"You didn't warn them about..." Sparky started but Dawn interrupted him immediately.

"Sometimes it's best not to know things Sparky."

CHAPTER 7

Sheriff Russell had finally tracked down his deputy, Raymond, retrieved the truck and gave him a dressing down, before storming off. But during his drive towards Pascoe's trailer, as he finished tuning his radio back to Radio Blackfoot again, he couldn't help but feel like a bit of a heel. He had really chewed out Raymond's ass and he felt a little bad about it, after the realisation sank in of where he had been. Unfortunately for Deputy Clegg this realisation didn't sink into Sheriff's Russell's head until he'd left.

"You're such an ass sometimes, Patrick. You know that?" He asked himself, not needing an answer to this particular question.

Deputy Raymond Clegg had become good friends with Chuck Muchnick and had been going to visit him every week since the ordeal that had happened just one year ago. The incident had really shook Chuck up and he no longer lived in the cabin that sat deep in the Maple Woods. He now rented a small trailer on the outskirts of Downtree, as far away from those woods as he could possibly get, without leaving Maple Falls altogether that is. Chuck had become a bit of a recluse and was hardly ever seen out of his trailer these days. Obviously people talk and gossiped about how 'Crazy' Chuck had finally completely lost it, openly mocking and laughing about his ordeal. The truth is it was fear that kept him hauled up in that trailer, fear of what lay out there in those woods, he knew exactly what was out there now and even though he knew that the town would be talking about him and making fun of him, he felt no comfort in how their lives hung by a thread. Raymond was the only one that was there for him, because he found him on that day, almost frozen in the wilderness, clutching onto an unconscious Professor Cumberbatch. He saw Chuck's fear, fear that seeped from his widened eyes and caked his face like a mask, a mask that he still wears today.

"You know that nobody goes to see poor old Muchnick anymore." Sheriff Russell said to himself "You know that Raymond's all he has!" He shook his head at his own insensitivity and thumped a leather gloved hand down on the steering wheel. "Damn it!"

He caught his reflection in the rearview mirror and sighed "You'll apologise to him when you get back to the office!" He said to his reflection and he nodded in agreement, he knew he'd been an ass, but sometimes the best thing a real man can do is apologise for the mistakes he'd made.

He shouldn't have yelled at him like that, especially when all he was doing was looking out for some strange old hermit that has nothing in his life. Maybe he shouldn't think of Chuck Muchnick like that, but having only been in Maple Falls for a short while all he had to go on was the town folk gossip. Also the incident report which really made no sense at all when reading through the events of that day. No new light had ever been shone on what happened in those woods, the statements from both men were nonsensical.

"Can't always believe the shit you hear, Patrick." He said to himself again as Dolly Parton's sweet Southern twang bled out of the speakers "Nope, sometimes you just have to make your own mind up about people."

The truck cut through the snow and into a part of town called Dekker. A random sprouting of trailer homes sat clustered around, all of them smothered in a layer of snow, they always looked like large shoe boxes to Sheriff Russell and that made him chuckle as he rolled up the gravelled path that cut through the site. Luckily some good Samaritan had been out with a snow shovel and removed the snow for any callers that may be visiting. The unknown shoveler had also been so kind as to cut out snaking pathways to each trailer, an admiral touch.

He pulled up outside Pascoe's trailer, their family name stuck on the side of the trailer next to the door in large fading stickers, one for each letter, slanted and crooked, as though they had been stuck up without much care. Sheriff Russell thought to himself that maybe Elroy stuck them up one night in a hurry after being fed up of hearing his wife nagging at him to get it done, and him making an half-assed attempt at the job, so she wouldn't ask him to do anything again. He chuckled to himself as he left the warmth of the truck slamming the door in his wake "Same thing I do at home when Holly wants me to do dishes. Half ass it, won't get asked again."

Marlena Pascoe was immediately up at the window at the sound of the door slamming. Sheriff Russell waved to her as he made his way down her newly shovelled pathway, snow piled up to his holster on either side. As he neared the entrance a frown fluttered across his brow when he saw how jittery Marlena looked. He knew that look, it was fear.

She opened the door before he could formally ring or knock, but she'd already seen him arrive anyway, so formality had been wained.

"Good afternoon, Mrs Pascoe!" Sheriff Russell smiled, removing his faux fur lined Ushanka style hat, sheriff badge pinned in the middle of it and gleaming from the lamplight coming from within the trailer.

"I take it, Elroy hasn't come home yet?"

"No!" She shrieked and with that started to cry.

"Okay, it's okay, Marlena." Sheriff Russell put his arm around her and entered the trailer closing the door behind them, hoping to stop any prying eyes from inquisitive neighbours that may have been peeping.

"Now, come on, you sit yourself down and tell me all about it." He said softly, handing her a tissue out of a fresh pack he always kept in his pocket. Not just for occasions like this, but since he'd been living here his nose would run like a son of a bitch, he wasn't yet fully acclimatised to the change in temperature from Crimson to Maple Falls. To him there was nothing worse (and unprofessional) than trying to deal with a situation with frozen nasal mucus stuck to his moustache.

Marlena sat on the worn threadbare sofa and dabbed at her tears with the tissue, trying to compose herself. Sheriff Russell sat on the edge of a bureau that homed a fruit bowl and an array of wildlife and hunting books that were randomly strewn on its scratched wooden surface. He toyed with his hat as he held it between his legs, he knew in this situation to not push the individual and allow them to come around when they were ready. He found this approach more effective when needing answers.

Marlena Pascoe was in her late fifties, but with her teary expression and obvious worry, she looked gaunt and about a decade older than her years. Even her once dark hair was now greying and looked tired as it was scooped up in a loose messy bun.

"I haven't heard from him since Friday, Sheriff." She sniffed.

"Where was he going, Marlena?"

"Maple Woods. He always calls me every night and he hasn't, and I can't get through to his cell, it's dead!"

"Any idea what area he would have gone to?"

"Well, he always follows Tear Drop Creek, parks up near Maple Cross and then goes by foot up to the woods"

"And what is he doing up there, Marlena?"

Marlena looked up at him, reluctant to answer him, for she knew just what he was getting at.

"Why was he up there?" He continued to probe, even though he already knew what the answer was "Can't do no fishing up there this time of year. Lake's frozen solid!"

She looked away, not able to make eye contact with him.

"He was out hunting, Sheriff." She sighed.

"I see." He replied with an apathetic rasp in his voice, as he placed his hat on the bureau and slowly zipped down his coat, removing a notebook, a pen already attached to it with its clip hugging the pads spiralling spine.

"I know it's wrong, Sheriff. I know that this time of year it's…"

"Illegal, Marlena! It's against the law!"

"I know." She sighed and her head dropped in self-pity and embarrassment "It's just… we need to live. Look around you, we're not living like no king and queen here!"

"I get that. I really sympathise with your situation, I really do. But, everyone is in the same boat. Elroy knows the season's dates and he knows it's against the law. He knows if he is caught he'd have to at least pay a hefty fine. He could even face some jail time!"

Marlena started to cry again, Sheriff Russell let her. He was mindful that although she may well be genuinely upset, there are some that use the waterworks to manipulate people, but, that wouldn't work on him.

After a couple of minutes he realised that her emotion was indeed genuine by the constant shaking of her chapped hands, this was no game to her, she was legitimately worried.

"Look, Marlena, I'll go up and see if I can find him. I've gotta take a trip up that way anyway."

"Would you!" She sniffed staring at him thankfully, with teardrops weighing down her dainty eyelashes.

"Of course!" He smiled "It's part of my job."

They smiled at each other and he jotted some notes down on his pad.

"So, his truck should be in Maple Cross, if he's hunting?"

"Yeah."

"And he always follows The Tear Drop Creek?"

"Yeah."

"Is there anything else you could tell me about his hunting patterns? Does he have any certain spots he likes to hit?"

"He tends to stay around, The Lumberjacks Cabins. Because well..." She looked up at him again with a look saying please forgive me "...he sometimes stays there overnight."

"Without Dawn's permission I take it?" He says shaking his head in disapproval.

She nods slowly, as she looks away again in embarrassment.

"What was he wearing when he left?"

"Oh, he always wears his white and grey camouflage all in one. Say's it's lucky. Always catches something when he wears it." She reminisced fondly "He said he became a ghost in that getup, that the animals could never see him in it."

"Okay." He nodded, but really he thought to himself *Oh, that's just fucking great! That'll make him easier to spot won't it.*

"What's his cell number and truck registration?"

"Oh I don't know off the top of my head, Sheriff. The truck is a black Dodge. That's all I know, I don't really now much about cars."

She grabs her cell, her hand shaking uncontrollably and jabs away with her index finger to find his number. She reads it out to him and he scribbles away frantically in his spidery handwriting that only he can read. Then he folds up his notepad, before slotting it back into the chest pocket of his shirt.

"If you could contact Lieutenant Adams at the office and let her know Elroy's truck registration if you find it."

"Yeah, sure!"

"I'll get out of your hair then" He said, fitting his hat back into place.

"Please find him, Sheriff." She sniffed.

"I'll do my utmost, Marlena. You hang in there."

And with a wink and a smile he left.

As he closed the door behind him, he could hear her sobs again, he sighed knowing that Elroy Pascoe had either left town or he was dead. That's what was usually the outcome in these matters.

CHAPTER 8

The snow that Dawn Rougeau promised had come early, and was already falling down around the eery Lumberjack cabin's plot as the visitors made their way slowly up the snow smothered dirt road.

Maple Woods stood silent, listening, waiting, as if it knew that there were guests arriving, and with this knowledge it was if Mother Nature had put plans into immediate effect for their imminent arrival.

There were several freshly trodden footprints in the surrounding area, they were curiously large, but undeniably had been man made. The impressions that had been made in the snow by some kind of hefty snow boot, had already started to fill up with the fresh thick flakes, as the relentless flurry fluttered silently through the gaping branches of the trees. Soon those footprints would be swallowed up and forgotten by the ongoing barrage of snow, leaving no evidence behind that they ever existed.

The curious footprints were not the only secrets being buried in the woods. Puddles of blood and small heaps of frozen viscera. The vibrant shades of reds, pinks and merlot splashed on a pure white canvas, like an abstract piece of art you would find in an art gallery by some eccentric artist. But now, that flamboyant splash of colour had gone, a crime scene left undiscovered, probably never to be solved, slid into a cold, dark body bag of concealment.

The large two floored cabins that sat dormant in the woods were made from the reddish grain of the Douglas fir, but in the early evening twilight they appeared almost black, dark and lifeless, like misshapen gravestones sprouting out of the snow.

The sound of a distant car engine disturbed the silent slumber of the Maple Woods, rumbling and coughing it was joined by the gnawing of its tyres through the deepening snow. Realising it could go no further it halted for a moment as if to calculate its next move, dual beams of saffron sliced through the white and black still life and lit up cabin number 3. The shadows of its curved windows gave the place an odd demeanour as though it was squinting in the light, it was almost as if it had not seen such brightness since the days of joy and merriment brought to it by the Tooth Family.

Knowing the van was defeated and could go no further through the deep snow it conceded and its engine was cut, leaving only the clinking and clunking sounds of the exhausted motor.

The guests burst out of the van from several exits in a hum of laughter and chatter, all of them carrying with them hefty bags, no doubt filled with warm clothing and private luxury possessions. The slamming and sliding of doors rattled through the trees and seemed to carry for miles as a spectrum of different coloured parkers all congregated outside the van together.

"I knew she'd get us here!" Quack said proudly, patting the warm hood of his trusty steed.

"Well, I for one am surprised." Scoffed Rob draping an arm around Sophie, "Fucking Shit coloured hunk of junk!"

"Cinnamon! She's cinnamon!" Quack growled, protectively.

"Whatever!" Rob scoffed rolling his eyes and forcing Sophie

69

up towards the cabin.

"Take no notice, Quack." Interrupted Jessica and gripped Quack by one of his chunky arms "If you'd be so kind to escort a lady to her quarters?"

"Of course!" He smiled and the two followed Rob and Sophie.

Max and Dustin looked at each other, both having the same idea before flashing identical cheesy grins towards Mia who stared at them with one eyebrow raised.

"Either one of you touch me and I'm breaking your arms." She sneered as she marched past them still clutching her book to her chest.

Max and Dustin shrugged at each other and held hands, and began to try and skip together through the snow unsuccessfully and immediately disappearing into the deep carpet of white in front of them. The group turned round to see what the commotion was all about and burst into fits of laughter as the duo popped up covered in snow, laughing hysterically themselves.

"Your friends are real dorks!" Rob sneered.

"I think you'll find we're all dorks here, quarterback!" Sophie exclaimed, as she brushed his arm away and bounded on through the snow ahead of him.

"Soph! I'm sorry, I didn't mean anything by it!" He pleaded as he tried to catch her up.

"Oh, oh! It would appear there is trouble in paradise already." Quack smirked.

"Now, now, Quack!" Jessica laughed.

Finally they all reached the cabin and Jessica let them inside. Rob was underwhelmed by the first look at the open plan downstairs room.

"Bit small isn't it?" He groaned, obviously used to more extravagant surroundings when he vacationed.

"What did you expect? The Ritz?" Quack blasted and switched on the light switch to get a better look at the place.

They all stood with snow falling off them, puddles around their wellington boots as they took in their surroundings, wall to wall wooden decor (as expected), large stone fire place, marble throughout the kitchen area and an array of decorative animal busts bursting through the walls.

"Oh my God!" Sophie shrieked, taken aback from the sights of foxes, cougars and racoon heads on the wall gawping at her, mouths gapping with teeth on show as if salivating on tasting the fresh flesh of these new visitors.

"Hey, it's got a table big enough for a Dungeon's and Dragon's session. So it's okay by me!" Smiled Dusty clapping his gloved hands before rubbing them together excitedly.

They dropped their bags by the door in the seven fresh puddles and went to explore.

Jessica approached the phone and perused the notepad with the information and the helpful numbers that Dawn had left for them in case of an emergency.

"There are four small bedrooms and a bathroom upstairs, and a log shed outback with enough logs for up to two weeks so we should at least be warm." Jessica smiled.

She then looked around and started taking charge of the sleeping arrangements. "So If I go with Mia, Dusty and Maximus..." They gave each other a high five "...Sophie you in with Rob, I take it?" Looking over at the couple who were still simmering from yet another disagreement.

"Yeah, sure I guess." She shrugs, Rob smiled, in his head thinking all sorts would be happening tonight.

"So that leaves Quack. You get the bridal suite all to yourself!"

"Cool." He smiled.

"Who'd want to share with that fucking walrus anyway." Murmured Rob, who was met with a vicious elbow from Sophie, who was luckily the only one who heard the unpleasant remark.

"Right, you kids go and explore and I'll go and get the groceries from the van." Quack said leaving the cabin.

"I'll give you a hand!" Jessica beamed and joined him back out in the cold while the others trudged upstairs to find their rooms.

CHAPTER 9

Sheriff Russell's truck cut through the snow of Maple Falls high street again, and through the rapid sweeping of the windshield wipers he noticed Deputy Raymond Clegg exiting Dawn's with a fresh coffee to go in his gloved hand. Hot steamy vapours escaped from the small opening in the cups lid and fought frivolously against the falling snow and freezing air. Sheriff Russell watched on and smirked as his Deputy's lips flickered and spasmed like a bad *Elvis Presley* impersonator, the heat scalding his chapped lips with every failed attempt to taste the hot coffee. He hit the siren for a quick sharp ear piercing blast, the sound causing Deputy Clegg to jump and drop his coffee into the snow covered sidewalk, the dark brownish liquid was hot and cut through the soft white snow like a stream.

"Oh, Goddamn it!" Deputy whined and stood rejected, just staring at the dark river that ran away from him.
Sheriff Russell pulled up along side of him and stepped out the out of the truck, a mischievous grin caressing his middle aged face, his thick grey moustache quivering as he fought to hold in the laughter.

"Had a little mishap there, Deputy?" He asked smiling.

"You got me good there, Sheriff! Real good!" Deputy Clegg nodded as he stooped down and picked up the now empty cup "I was looking forward to that too. The Joe at the office tastes like moose piss!" He sighed dropping the cup and lid into a nearby trashcan.

Sheriff laughed as he slammed the door behind him and approached him slapping a hand on his rejected slouched shoulders "C'mon, I'll buy you another one." He smiled and the two of them walked into Dawn's.

"You back again so soon, Raymond?" Dawn asked in surprise as she cleaned down the counter in an empty diner.

"Yeah, I dropped the little bugger on the sidewalk." Deputy Clegg sighed.

"Oh, that's too bad!" Sympathised Dawn.

"It was totally my fault." Sheriff Russell intervened "Can I get him another one please, Dawn?"

"Sure!" Dawn said looking up at the clock on the wall surrounded by old vintage sepia toned photographs of what Maple Falls used to look like. "You've just beaten the clock, I'm about to close up for the day."

"Well, we appreciate that, Dawn." Sheriff said with a smile, removing his hat and plonking it down on the counter, as Dawn set about making another coffee for Deputy Clegg. "Actually, could you make it two, Dawn?"

"Sure thing!" She replied.

"Thanks for the coffee, Sheriff." Grinned the goofy Deputy.

"Hey, it was my fault, scaring you like that. Everybody seems to be a bit jumpy round here lately!" Stated Sheriff Russell rubbing his hand across his stubbled chin.

Dawn and Raymond share a look that the Sheriff didn't see or if he did, he didn't acknowledge it.

"Just that winter feeling I guess, Sheriff." Deputy Clegg

shrugs and smiles an awkward smile. "Gets colder and darker. Spookier I guess!"

"Yeah, If you say so." Sheriff shrugs back, his mind seems to be miles away, as if thinking of something.

"You okay, Sheriff?"

"Huh!" Sheriff grunts snapping back to reality. "Oh, yeah! Just miles away I guess. I'm actually glad I caught up with you, as I wanted to say sorry about how I snapped at you earlier."

"Oh, there's no need to apologise, Sheriff. I shouldn't have taken the truck again without asking."

"No, I overreacted."

They smiled at each other as their coffees arrived.

"There you go, you two degenerates. Now get outta here and let this lady get home at a respectable time for once!" Dawn chirped.

They grabbed their coffees and thanked Dawn and headed for the door.

"You go to see that Muchnick character quite a lot don't ya, Raymond?" Asked Sheriff Russell, his turn to tentatively stab a lip at the hot coffee cup.

"Yeah... Well, he's got nobody else to visit him you see. It's my duty..."

"No, it's more than your duty, Raymond!" He interrupted "You're going above and beyond for him, and I commend you for that." Sheriff Russell smiled at him and patted him on the back.

"Wow, thanks, Sheriff!" Deputy Clegg said proudly.

"I actually would like to meet the fellow and ask him some questions myself."

Deputy Clegg reached for the door handle and stopped dead

in his tracks.

"Really?" Clegg stuttered and sheepishly looked over at Dawn, this time Sheriff Russell noticed the strange eye contact between the two in the reflection of the window. It was curious moments like this that made Sheriff Russell believe that there was more to Maple Falls than just ghost stories and Blackfoot myths. Something had happened here that made the whole town put up their defences in the winter time. This was his first winter at Maple Falls and he had noticed the change in peoples demeanour, it was all very bizarre. He felt that people were whispering behind his back, keeping a secret from him, one that they all shared apart from him.

I'm an outsider.

I guess he'll always be seen as an outsider.

"What about?" Clegg asked "I can tell you all you need to know about him." He added trying to smile and act natural, but it wasn't working, he was hiding something and Sheriff Russell knew it. But he wasn't about to let on that he knew something was wrong, so he played dumb. He played along with whatever this charade was.

"Oh, I'm working through those old files trying to draw a line under them." His eyes flitting from his Deputy's face to Dawn's reflection, both of them now wearing uncharacteristic masks of anxiety, as though they were about to throw up. It looked as though they'd seen a ghost.

"Yeah! The one about Muchnick and the Professor? The 'supposed' yeti attack." He laughed it off and Clegg and Dawn both followed suit with jitters of forced laughter.

"So, do you think you could arrange a meeting between us?" Deputy Clegg's eyes flitted back to Dawn as he searched for a reply,

76

her head dropped slightly and she nodded to him.

"Yeah! Yeah I'm sure I could do that for you, Sheriff!" He smiled.

"Good!" Sheriff Russell announced and ushered his Deputy out of the door "Now, c'mon, we've taken up enough of Dawn's time. She has a home to get to you know!"

Dawn stood by the counter wringing her cloth so tightly in her laboured hands that they had turned white. As Sheriff turned to say goodnight to her he spotted his hat on the counter. He approached the counter to retrieve it.

"Blasted hat." He smiled at Dawn.

"Sheriff?" She murmured.

"Yes, Dawn?" He frowned as she approached him.

"I....erm..." She struggled for the words she wanted to say, her eyes looking into his and then over at Deputy Clegg in the doorway "I..." She tried, but still the words would not come, it was although they were being held prisoner in her larynx, unable to escape.

"Yes, Dawn I'm listening?" And with that he held her hand over the counter, her grip loosening on the cloth with his touch and she looked into his eyes, he could see that something was in there, something that so needed to be said, but she couldn't and different words came out.

"Did you visit those kids at the cabin yet?" The thought had totally slipped his mind.

"No! No Dawn I haven't."

He smiled a smile that was meant to put her mind at rest.

"I'll go up there now before it get's too dark, and before

another flurry of this shit."

She grabbed his hand and held them tightly, so tightly that it was his hand that was turning white now, having all the colouring wrung from it like water from a sponge.

"Please be careful of those woods, Sheriff." She said quietly, a nervous quiver in her voice "It's winter remember!" and with that statement her eyes grew wide as if they yearned to scream that secret to him. He knew there was some subliminal message there for him to take on, but he didn't know what it was. He smiled and pulled his hand out of her grip and gently put his hand on top of hers and patted it.

"I appreciate your concern, Dawn. But I don't believe in any of that superstition mumbo jumbo." And with that, dumped his hat back on his head and left the diner with an anxious Deputy in tow.

As the door shut behind them, Dawn was left alone. She gazed trancelike at the wall of old photographs and murmured the words under her breath.

"I don't believe in that either...Sheriff."

CHAPTER 10

Cabin number 3 is all lit up, bathing its deep white surroundings with several beams of light, changing the snows appearance to the subtleness of a pale daffodil. With life being breathed into the forgotten structure it acts like a beacon in the cold dark woods, as if beckoning someone.

The snow continues to fall in large chunks, and with darkness consuming the woods that eery silence returns, where there is no sound, nothingness. Through the dark rising foliage that sprouts out in all directions, a figure observes. The stranger remains hidden in shadow and quietly observes the recent arrivals. Only the shallow breaths and escaping clouds of warm air rising into the falling flakes gives his position away. But there is nobody looking, nobody suspecting.

The figure's curiosity prevails, disregarding what it did to the cat, and the figure advances through the snow clad shrubbery with cumbersome reckless abandon, disturbing the accumulation of hours of snowfall that had settled on branches. The hefty figure lumbered through the snow towards the cabin, aware enough to stay in the shadows.

The breathing was heavy, gruff and masculine. Worn and tattered working boots, splattered with all manner of unidentifiable stains trample the carpet of virgin snow, with no regard for its beauty as he reaches the cabin. He glares through a side window, unseen, gently his ripe breath kisses the window pane and it mists over, but only for seconds before it dissolves and is replaced in a constant sequence as he scrutinised what was playing out inside.

Laughter and friendly chattering rose from the long eight place oak table, where the new arrivals had settled in and were enjoying some of Quack's homemade macaroni and cheese. A speciality of the chef who had added a succulent layer of ground beef underneath the piping hot 'Mac n Cheese'. The meal was accompanied by a large bowl of moist salad that was being passed around from person to person, all of them grabbing at their chosen vegetables with snapping tongs. The bowl ending back where it had begun in front of Jessica, who having already partaken positioned the bowl back in the centre of the table.

Chester Duckworth (or 'Quack' to his friends) tucked into his meal, his plate very light on the salad. He nodded and smiled proudly taking in all the adulation his fine meal had conjured up.

Jessica Head sat to his right and looked at him fondly, she was pretty and wore her fiery hair in matching pigtails. She picked at the meal with her folk daintily.

Next to her was Mia Chung, she was enjoying the meal and the conversation, her serious face cracking on occasion and flashing a smile. She was a good eater and enjoyed her food and only stopped cramming more of Quack's delicious meal into her mouth when she felt the need to push her sliding glasses back up her nose. Her book sat next to her plate, it had not left her side since piling into Quack's van back in Studd City.

Maximus Fellows bellowed loudly with laughter, showing the cluster of chewed up macaroni, cheese and beef, it wasn't good table manners and not a pretty sight for the others to endure, but they laughed because they loved Max, he was always the life and soul of the party.

Robbie Guy did not find Max's disgusting table manners funny, nor his inside jokes about *Dungeons and Dragons*, he especially thought that his constant impression of *Yoda* from *Star Wars* was awful too. He didn't fit in with these types of people and if he were honest, he was only here because he thought he had a chance of fucking Sophie Hewitt. But, unfortunately for him, she had other plans. She listened and laughed at the conversation and looked very interested in what Quack had to say as he described the recipe for what he called 'Quack n' Mac'! She always listened to what people had to say and loved a discussion. She had the looks of a cheerleader with her slender figure and pert breasts crowned with long straight golden hair. But losing her virginity on this week's excursion was not on the cards.

Dustin Greaves soon realised that the joke was on him when he attempted to start a food fight with his partner in crime, Max, by using his fork as a catapult and launching a chunky piece of melted cheese into the air, only for it to propel itself backwards and land in his short dark curly hair. The table erupted at such a sight and with that the figure moved away from the window.

Quack leant back in his chair full and content and slapped his hands on his large belly, it shook under his ill fitting shirt. "Well, I'm full!" He announced.

"I fucking doubt it!" Rob scoffed under his breath, which wasn't heard under the ruckus of cutlery clattering against the empty plates. Sophie heard it though, and gave him a sharp kick under the table that struck his shin and caused him to wince, before he could say anything she cut him a look. Rob decided to quit why he was ahead and say nothing, knowing that upsetting her now could affect his goal of scoring later on.

"Really great meal, Quack!" Sophie said smiling at Quack who blushed a little, but smiled back.

"So what's the plan for tonight?" Quack asked clapping his hands together "I know Maximus and Big Dust have brought Dungeons and Dragons!" He said hopefully, and enthusiastically, but also knowing that the girls may not want to partake.

"Yes!" Came the cry in unison from Dustin and Max slapping a high five over the table and knocking into Mia.

"Watch it!" She groaned.

Jessica stood up and started to clear the plates from the table, "First thing's first. Let's wash these dishes and then we can talk about what's on the cards."

There was an unanimous petulant groan from the group, but they still followed suit clearing up.

When Quack saw Sophie carrying a number of items towards the kitchen, he attempted to get up and help "Here, let me help you, Soph!"

She smiled and rested a free hand on his shoulder and said, "Now, you sit yourself down. You've cooked us all a lovely meal. No dishes for you!" and with that she walked away towards the kitchen. Quack couldn't help himself but look at her bottom as it swayed hypnotically under a cotton dress.

Rob had been watching and approached him while everyone else was busy taking things to the kitchen. He grabbed his shoulder and squeezed it hard, Quack turned to face him and Rob scowled at him whispering venomously "I can see what you're doing fat boy and you've got no fucking chance!"

Quack scowled back and was about to say something when his feelings were crushed with one statement that may have been the truth.

"She'd never be interested in an ugly fat piece of shit like you!" Hissed Rob loosening his grip on Quack's shoulder and patting him on the back just as Sophie turned around.

"Thanks for the chow, big man!" Rob smiled and Sophie smiled back, genuinely thinking that they were making the effort to get a long with each other.

At that moment Quack could have cried but he obviously didn't, he couldn't show the hurt in front of the others, especially not in front of him.

Jessica washed the dishes in the sink and Max dried unenthusiastically.

"So what's the plan tonight guys? What are we gonna do?" Jessica called from the sink.

Mia shuffled across the room and scooped up her book from the table "Well, I'm going to read my book!" and with that collapsed into a comfy looking chair next to the roaring open fire, wrapping herself in one of the many fur skins that were draped over the back of the chair.

"Oh, what a surprise!" Announced Dustin sarcastically rolling his eyes at her. She scrunched up her face towards him in an act of defiance.

"And I was going to tell you all about my Pro Wrestling trading card collection!" Dustin said excitedly sitting awkwardly on the arm of the chair.

"Oh the joys!" Came the sarcastic response from Mia as she opened up her book again. But before she could settle down into the escapism of her favourite magical world, something made her turn to her left and she was met by the head of a deer, she screamed, dropping her book on the ground. Max started laughing as he came out from behind the chair with the deer's head that he'd snatched from the wall. Mia clutched her chest as it heaved rapidly.

"Jack ass!" She shouted picking up the weighty book and hitting him with it.

"Oh! 'Deer' me! I am sorry!" Max chuckled and then chased Dustin around the table with the head, trying to gore him with its dusty antlers.

"I'm going to get Dungeons and Dragons!" Dustin yelled as he ran up the stairs followed closely by Max with the deers head singing "Doe, a deer, a female deer..." as he gave chase.

"Well, I guess it's dungeons and Dragons then." Jessica smiled wiping her hands.

"You're going to play?" Quack chirped up surprised.

"Sure, why not!" Jessica answered "I'll even make us some cocoa while you guys set things up!"

"What a woman!" Quack laughed, and truth be told a little turned on by the fact she wanted to join them.

"Well, I'm going to get an early night. I am beat!" Sophie announced and headed for the stairs. Rob smirked and looked at Quack.

"Yeah! Me too!"

"Goodnight all!" Sophie announced and was met by a unison of goodnights.

Quack watched Sophie walk up the stairs and even the glimpse of her slender thigh couldn't lighten the dark mood that he felt inside.

"Robbie Guy, I hope you fucking die a horrible death!" He murmured to himself as he watched his grinning face disappear up the stairs.

CHAPTER II

It was 9:30pm when Sheriff Russell finally made it to where the dirt road cut into the Maple Woods usually was situated, now it was smothered in a deep carpet of snow. Amazingly only a few hours earlier he would have found the treads from a few *Goodyear's* etched into it, but their existence was long gone now. He had to park on the road as there was no way he'd get the truck up to the cabins in that amount of snow, even if he could, he didn't think he'd be able to get back. Tomorrow would be time to break out the Bobcat's he thought, it was too deep for the trucks now and it was officially snowmobile weather. Secretly he'd been wishing for the chance to take one out for a spin, now he would get the chance, he smiled as he looked up the long pathway into the darkness and was suddenly frozen by a tingling shudder that ran the length of his spine, but it wasn't the cold that caused the shudder, he couldn't actually put his finger on what had caused it, it was a surreal feeling almost like a vulnerable feeling, almost like fear.

A gargantuan snowplough hurtled passed on Maple Way behind him, beeping its horn loudly at him, almost causing him to jump out of his socks, lose his lunch and shit himself all at the same time.

"Bastard!" He whined as he composed himself. He put that strange feeling and thoughts of fear to the back of his mind and he started to walk up towards the cabins.

He struggled through the deep snow, the icy sting working up his legs to his thighs, in that moment of clarity he'd promised himself he would be quick, get in, check on them and get the fuck out. It was too cold to be messing around. His eyes danced between the pillars of trees looking out into the darkness beyond, he felt that fear again, everywhere he looked he was surrounded by the same towering redwoods caked in thick layers of snowfall, and the flakes that fell danced around his peripherals causing him to see things in the dark that weren't really there. Or was there something there? Using the cascading snowflakes as a distraction! Somewhere in the vast woodland abyss, a branch snapped and halted him. He stood in the thigh high snow statue still and motionless, not even wanting to blink, as the soft cold flakes congregated on his eyelashes. Suddenly the call of a Great Horned Owl warbled through the air, seemingly coming from all around him as it called to its mate. He shuddered and sighed a shaky sigh of relief as he heard its wings flap as it rose into the sky somewhere unseen.

He carried onwards, swallowing hard he decided to try and take his mind off his actual whereabouts and he remembered a conversation he'd had with his wife before he'd made the drive up to the woods.

He was always late home, so it had come as no surprise to Holly Russell who had settled down in front of the television for the evening with a mug of hot cocoa. She often had to slide her husband's dinner into the oven on a low heat to keep it warm, tonight it was half a dish of Pâté Chinois that had found it's way in there, Holly could wait no longer and had eaten her share, done the dishes and had a hot soak in the tub. Now it was time for a horror movie marathon that was just starting on CanTV. The channel was showing some classic *Hammer* movies from the 60's and 70's. Tonights terrifying trifecta were, *The Devil Rides Out, The Brides of Dracula* and *Scars of Dracula*. Patrick thought it was all trash, but she loved those old British classics, especially when Christopher Lee was involved.

The dirging sound of *The Devil Rides Out's* chilling introduction played as she snuggled down under a blanket on the armchair. She wrapped her hands around her warm mug as a background of claret danced yellow pentagrams and then Beelzebub himself filled the screen, her cell rang and caused her to spill the cocoa on herself "Shit!" She said wiping her hands and answering the phone "Your timing is impeccable as usual, Pat!" She groaned down the phone.

"What did I do know?" Sighed Sheriff Russel playfully.

"Nothing just spilt my drink. What's up?"

"I'm afraid I'm going..."

"Too be late?" She intervened "Pat, it's 9 o'clock. I kind of figured!"

"Sorry."

"I'm used to it now." She smiled, she knew what the deal was when you were married to a man of the law.

"I won't be too long, I had totally forgotten to go and check on those college kids that are staying out at one of the cabins in the woods."

"Funny time of the year to have the cabins occupied, isn't it?"

"Yeah, I thought that too. But, I think Dawn is struggling for cash at the moment, so she's opened them up for the winter too."

"Fair enough I guess."

"Yeah, so I'm hoping not to be too long."

"Well, you just be careful out there. Don't like the thought of you out in the woods at night!"

"Yeah, Me neither!" He laughed "I'll be as quick as I can."

"Oh, Take your time!" she said smiling as suave goateed Christopher Lee strutted onto screen and shook hands with a very young looking Patrick Mower.

"Gee thanks..." then the realisation hit him and he laughed "Christopher Lee?"

"Yep!" She giggled.

"Enjoy!" He chuckled.

"Don't let that Blackfoot get ya!"

That last sentence would normally have been laughed off, and at the time around 40 minutes ago it was, but now, deep in the woods alone, Sheriff Russell wasn't laughing.

The more he gazed into that nothingness and the more he heard those strange sounds of nocturnal creatures going about their routines, the quicker the cogs turned in his head. They turned and turned and made his eyes see things that may not have been there. Shapes moving in between the trees, or sounds that he may not have heard, growls and howls and shrieks. At one point he thought he heard a scream, but again he tried not to overanalyse what could have been the gargle of a wolverine or the shrilling of a buzzard, the mind can play tricks on oneself if one lets it. Or at least that's what he told himself.

At last he saw light up ahead and he sighed thankfully, knowing he could now focus on something else.

CHAPTER 12

Dungeon master Max had just announced that Quack, Jessica and Dustin's battling barbarians were now trapped in a dark, damp repugnant cave. The half eaten remains of the last failing tribe scattered on the bloodstained floor, when suddenly they are surrounded by "Goblins!" He cackled rubbing his hands together sadistically.

"Goblins again!" Groaned Quack.

"What?" Max asks with all sincerity.

"What's the matter with goblins?" Asked the rookie participant Jessica.

"It's alway fucking goblins!" Dustin sighed before head butting the table in a moment of slapstick exasperation.

"What's the big deal?" Asked Max.

"Well, it's not very original is it Max?" Quack says shrugging.

"It's always goblins with you Maximus!" Dustin says, head rising from the table, a spell card stuck to his clammy forehead "Couldn't you make it a Cyclops or Harpies, or anything! Just for a change?"

"Fine!" Scoffs a now disgruntled Dungeon Master "A leopard print Super-fly Cadillac springs into the cave! You are now surrounded by a group of 1970s Harlem pimps! Wielding sword canes and a bubbling purple poison spilling from their chalices!"

There is a moment of silence as they all just stare at Max blankly. He stares back at them waiting in anticipation.

Finally Quack speaks, calmly "I don't think you're taking this seriously."

The table erupts with laughter.

Mia sits cocooned in fur on the chair, book hanging loosely in her grip as she gawks at them in confusion.

"You guys are insane!" She says shaking her head before it burrows back into the worn yellowing pages of her book.

The laughter was short lived when the bellowing of Robs voice came sweeping down the staircase on a waft of angry obscenities. The game and book reading stopped as everyone gazed up at the stairs, a door slammed jolting the log structure so much that the hunters mounts rattled from side to side, as if they were shaking their lifeless heads in disapproval.

Rob bounded down the stairs, each angry stomp attacking the wooden steps beneath his heavy duty all-weather boots. His face glowing with a mixture of anger and embarrassment, he launched his holdall down the stairs and it landed with a thump. He muttered some incoherent words under his breath as he wildly knitted the buttons on his checked shirt back together. Mia's eyebrows rose and hovered over the round lenses of her glasses as she caught a glimpse of his chiseled physique.

"That fucking bitch!" Rob growled as he reached the main room of the cabin.

Quack immediately shot up from his chair as if he'd been electrocuted, his large podgy hands squeezed tightly into fists.

Rob stopped and looked at him, still buttoning his shirt. "You got something to say Fat boy?" He sneered.

"If you've hurt her, I'll..." Quack began to say before being interrupted by Rob.

"Oh you can cool your jets! I haven't fucking hit her!"

Jessica rose and held onto Quack's chunky arm to try and calm him down, it worked, his fists loosened.

"Calm down Quack!" She whispered calmingly.

"Yeah you listen to her. You don't want to embarrass yourself now do you?" Rob added before stomping across towards the couch, where their coats all lay piled up on and began rummaging through them all until he found his bright orange Parker.

Yet again he growled obscenities and harshness as his Parker became stuck on something and he angrily tugged at it. It tore as it came bursting out of the mountain of colourful coats, causing several items from the coat pockets to spill (including Dustin's wrestling card collection) onto the wooden panel flooring.

"Hey!" Dustin yelled.

His defiant cry was soon extinguished by Rob's furious stare. He gazed at his Parker that was now discharging a mass of goose feathers from its fresh wound and screamed "For fuck's sake!"

Quack found pleasure in this and an uncontrollable smirk twitched between his podgy cheeks.

"Oh you're laughing at me now fat boy?You think this is funny?" He seethes taking several strides towards the table, his coat gripped in his hand.

"I'm not fucking scared of you, asshole!" Quack growled back at him with such conviction in his eyes that it halted Rob. They glared at each other in an intense stare down, neither of them looking like they were going to concede.

Max leaned over to Dustin very slowly and whispered "This is like watching Hogan and The Giant at Mania III!"

Dustin didn't answer, but he slowly nodded, his eyes fixated at the two towering titans that stood before them.

"Fine!" Rob said finally, and knowing that Quack was willing to fight for Sophie's reputation he was the one to back down, but not before whipping his Parker across the table and destroying their game in the process.

"You want to be her knight in shining armour, then be my guest!" Rob said stomping towards his discarded holdall and scooping it up by one of its handles.

"She's nothing but a fucking cock teaser!" He growled looking up at the stairs and seeing Sophie wrapped in a thick dressing gown, with tears in her eyes. He stopped for a second looking at her, a moment of clarity maybe seeping through the red haze, but then a glance at the others and his ego would not allow it. "I'm outta here!" He shouted before storming out of the cabin into the cold night, the thick wooden door slamming behind him.

"What a fucking prick!" Max said shaking his head.

"Why didn't you tell him that two minutes ago, Maximus?" Dustin enquired.

"I was about to!" He sniggered.

Quack, Jessica and Mia made for the stairs as an upset Sophie shuffled down them.

"Are you okay, Soph? What did that bastard do to you?" Quack asked.

93

"Nothing! He didn't do anything to me." She sniffed.

"Then what's going on?" Jessica asked rubbing her arm.

"He thought I'd asked him to come along because I was going to put out." She snivelled "He just got angry when I told him I still wasn't ready yet."

"I'm gonna kill him!" Quack growled and made for the door until he was stopped by Max and Dustin.

"Calm down, big man!" Dustin said.

"Violence never solved anything." Max added with a wag of his finger which made Quack laugh and seemed to snap him out of doing anything rash.

"You're probably, right."

"So where has he gone?" Mia asked "It's freezing out there!"

"He's probably just gone to let off some steam, he'll be back within the hour I'm sure." Jessica smiled, reassuring Sophie who although very upset by the whole ordeal, still had feelings for Rob.

"I don't know." Sophie said shaking her head "He said he was leaving!"

"Well, then that's his own stupid idea. If he wants to go, let him go!" Quack said returning to the table and picking up all the debris from their game.

"If he's damaged any of my collection I'll snap him!" Dustin sneered picking up the flayed out cards.

"You couldn't snap your fingers!" Max mocked as he picked up the parkers that had fallen to the floor.

Jessica hugged Sophie.

"You want to come and join us down here?" Jessica asked, but she declined with a shake of her head "No thanks, Jess. I think

I'm going to go and get some sleep."

"Do you want me to fix you up a cocoa?" Jessica asked.

Sophie nodded and smiled.

"C'mon, let's get you to bed!" Mia said as she helped her upstairs and Jessica walked towards the kitchen area. She stopped behind Quack, who was busily picking items up from the floor and trying to remember where certain pieces were. She smiled lovingly at him and caressed her hand softly over his wide back, he turned to look at her and their eyes met. Quack's eyebrows rose as if hit with a sudden moment of clarity. She smiled at him "Our hero!" She grinned before walking towards the kitchen.

Quack stood there frozen as he watched Jessica swinging her bubble butt from side to side as she walked away.

"Damn!" He murmured, he had never looked at her that way because they'd always been such good friends and she'd always been like one of the guys. A new light was shining on her now and when she looked over her shoulder and they made eye contact again, he knew that there was something special there. Maybe it had always been there hidden in plain sight.

CHAPTER 13

Rob was still spewing profanity as he bounded outside, the cold immediately smacked him in the face with a flurry of falling snow attached to it and he was swiftly brought back to reality.

"Fuck, it's cold!" He said shivering and dropping his bag in the deep snow, as he hurried into his Parker. The bright orange jacket stood out in the whiteness, he looked like a giant traffic cone when he pulled his hood up into place. He sighed as he stood there in the snow, he knew he should probably go back in and apologise, at least he'd be in the warmth. But yet again his ego wouldn't allow it. He thought about walking to the town, but a look at the increasingly deepening snow that lay ahead made him change his mind. He looked down at his holdall, becoming speckled in a peppering of soft snowflakes and not wanting it to get ruined or buried he picked it up and walked back over to the front door of the cabin.

Next to the cabin stood a garbage can which was crowned with a large lefty brick, obviously put there as a Racoon deterrent. He lifted the brick off and opened the can, which was empty as no one had stayed there for a while. He hauled his holdall up and dropped it into the can. He put the lid back in place and then topped it off with the brick. Sighing again, he stood thinking about what to do next. The wind blew and he shivered, he had definitely realised that he didn't want to be stuck out in this, no, he'd have a cigarette and mull things over before going back in and eating some humble pie.

He slid out the packet of half empty Freebirds from his Parker pocket and placed it between his quivering lips, if anything he thought it might warm him up a little. He struck a match and suckled on mistress nicotine inhaling deeply. He already felt a lot better as he launched the smouldering match into the unforgiving snow, where it sizzled and died in a shroud of smoke.

As he began to walk around the cabin, slowly and cumbersome in the deep snow he reflected, talking out loud to get his point across.

"Hey, I know I can be an asshole, nobody's gotta tell me that! But aren't we all sometimes?" There was a pause as he took another drag of the cigarette, the burning embers flickering in the darkness.

"No! I'm not at fault here, why blame yourself! It's that fucking slut in there!"

He knew this was bullshit as he stomped away from the cabin toward a fallen tree he had spotted rising from the mounds of fallen snow. She wasn't a slut, if she was then he wouldn't be out here in the cold now, sucking on a cigarette talking to himself.

"You could have any girl you like!" He told himself as he sat down on the fallen tree.

"Heck, you've had most of them!" He smiled and enjoyed his Freebird, reminiscing about conquests of the past. None of them had ever complained, he was good at sex, had a great physique and a generous slab of girth hanging between his legs "What girl wouldn't want that combination?" he nodded to himself, he sniggered at the thought of having a large dick, because at the moment it felt like the size of a walnut whip!

97

"No, she played you buddy. She enticed you to come here with her boring nerdy friends and spend the week with her. Knowing all along that there was no way she was going to put out!" He exhaled again and watched as the smoke danced in the darkness, lit only by the light from the cabin. A snapping twig from somewhere out in the woods broke his train of thought and he looked out into the darkness, waiting to hear it again. He didn't hear it again and he turned his attention back to the cabin and then looked down at his cigarette. He knew he was being a dick over all of this like a toddler throwing his pacifier out of the crib because he didn't get his own way. He just couldn't bring himself to say it.

"Rob you're a fucking as..." He was stopped mid sentence by the snapping of another twig, but this time it came from right behind him. He turned around expecting to see darkness but instead was met by a dirty stained checked shirt. Confusion cavorted across his brow "What the..." he began but was struck mute when his gaze ascended to the shirts wearer and was met by a gigantic bearded face staring back at him, protrusions etched into his balding head, and scarred knots bulging from it giving him the appearance of an old potato.

"Who the fuck are you?" Rob managed to splutter.
The stranger grinned, showing a maw with very few incisors. The ones he did have were broken or cracked like the tusks of a battle worn boar. He didn't answer Rob, but instead just laughed. It was a deep and low sound, the kind of sound you'd make if you wanted to clear your throat. Saliva hung from the broken shards of left over teeth and actually dripped onto Rob's face.

"What the fuck!" He growled, getting pissed off but still not computing that he was at risk and he stood up wiping the spittle from his face and flinging his cigarette away, readying himself for a tussle. But as he stood and turned around fully he saw the gargantuan size of the man that stood before him, he was more like a grizzly bear that had risen on its hind legs. He looked into the dark sockets where his eyes should be but he didn't see eyes, he saw death. And then it finally dawned on him that he was in trouble when he saw the axe that was hanging down by his side and the freshly sharpened blade winking at him from the illuminating light of the cabin.

"Shit!" He managed before running towards the cabin. It was a struggle to move quickly through the snow, he made the mistake of trying to lift his feet out each time to try and run, instinctively, what anyone would do in the same situation. He got nowhere fast and the stranger was gaining on him. Looking over his shoulder Rob saw that the man, or beast, or whatever it was, was not stepping but just pushing himself through the snow, almost shuffling but it helped him move faster. Rob tried it and managed to move ahead of him. Suddenly he tripped spilling into the snow, he looked behind him to see what he had fallen over and frowned again with confusion when he saw "Trip wire?"

By the time he had realised, the area had obviously been boobytrapped and it was too late as the beast was on him.

He stood towering over him drooling sadistically and brought the axe up over his head, it seemed to hover there for several minutes but in fact it was only a second or two before it was brought crashing down.

The axe hit the frozen dirt beneath the snow as it sprayed off in multiple directions. He looked up to see Rob up again and making for the cabin. Rob was an Allstar in college, he was on his way to the big leagues of football and had already had been in talks to join Studd City Sharks in the PBFL when he graduated, so to say he was quick was an understatement. But the axe wielding ogre remained still and no longer gave chase as Rob had once again managed to get to his feet and headed quickly towards the cabin. Had he given up or was this a perverted way of playing with his prey? Rob looked around and slowed down realising that the beast was no longer following him, all he saw was the large irregular silhouette standing in the distance.

"What the fuck is this?" Rob panted as he had once again taken his eye off his whereabouts. He stopped for a moment staring at the stranger before turning to run again. It was then that his foot was snagged by another tripwire, but this time he was propelled towards the ground and the last thing he ever heard was the loud metallic biting of a bear trap, which lay in wait concealed by a dusting of snow.

Rob's body squirmed for a few moments as blood oozed out around the closed jaws of the trap. Rob's hand came up and flailed away aimlessly at the side of the trap, staining his fingers with thick oozing plasma that seeped continuously from the wound. Finally his hand went limp and it fell into the snow, blotching the whiteness with violent flecks of red. There was a sickening sound of crunching bone as his bodyweight forced his head to slide off the grinning bloodied jowl of the trap, his body coming to settle in the cold snow. All that could be heard now was the subtle sliding of the strangers mass as it waded through the snow towards his prize, resembling an enormous

100

hungry orca.

He stood above the lifeless body and there was a satisfied sigh and a vulture grunt of amusement as he assessed his artistry. Rob's face had been completely consumed by the bear trap, leaving behind a broken crater, laden with a grisly splintered bouquet of flesh and bone.

CHAPTER 14

The barrage of falling snow had stopped by the time Sheriff Russell reached cabin number 3. He was very relieved to reach the cabin, to see it all lit up and alive warmed his frost bitten heart. Finally he could relax and not worry about what may or may not be laying in wait for him amidst the tall dark redwoods.

As he approached the cabin he noticed some very large footprints that disappeared around the rear of the building. He decided to just take a wander around the property, just to make sure everything was okay. He followed them, a leather gloved hand loosely gripping the office issue Glock 17's plastic handle, just in case. As quietly as he could he moved around the building following the trail. All he found was a small woodshed. The trail did not lead to the small structure and instead carried on around the cabin, so he carried on. He completed a full circuit of the cabin and found nothing but the front door, back where he started. He thankfully removed his hand from the handle of his firearm and knocked on the door. The door was opened by Jessica, now wrapped in a thick dressing gown and a fresh mug of cocoa warming her free hand.

"Oh, Hi!" Jessica said a little startled but still pleasant, as always. "Is everything okay?" She then asked seriously.

"Good Evening, folks!" Sheriff Russell said, the words escaping his mouth on a wave of mist and on seeing this, Jessica ushered him in side "Where are my manners! Do forgive me Sheriff. You must be freezing!"

"Thank you kindly Miss!" He smiled taking off his hat that disturbed a thick layer of snow that had built up on his trek, the snow hit the floorboards and immediately began to melt from the warmth in the room.

"Is everything okay?" Quack said rising from his chair at the table.

"Please don't get up!" The Sheriff gestured raising his hand at him and shaking his head "It's just a routine check. I promised Dawn...I mean, Ms Rougeau that I would check to see if you guys were all fine and dandy." He smiled, his icicle lacquered moustache cracking as he did so "All part of the service." He laughed.

A communal sigh of relief filled the air and everyone smiled, realising that everything was fine.

"Go ahead and warm yourself by the fire, Sheriff." Jessica offered.

"I think I'll take you up on that Miss." The Sheriff nodded and walked over to the fireplace, taking in his surroundings the way an officer of the law would.

"How long have you been out there?" Max piped up and asked as The Sheriff stood warming himself in front of the raging flames.

"Oh! About an hour or so!"

"It's a wonder you're not frozen solid!" Max replied shaking his head in disbelief.

"Made of stronger stuff out this way aren't you, Sheriff?" Quack smiled.

"Something like that!" Sheriff nodded "But, I'm not from Maple Falls originally. I'm a Sanctuary City boy myself. But, it's just as harsh up there. Thickens the blood, my old man used to say." He laughed and then stopped, realising these kids probably didn't want to hear about his past.

"Can I get you anything Sheriff?"
He looked at the steaming mug of cocoa in her hand, it looked so inviting to him.

"No!" He said, kicking himself "I don't want to put you out."

"No, it's fine!" Jessica smiled "I've got a thermos around here, I'll make some up for your journey back."

"Oh there's really no need, Miss!" He pleaded.

"I insist!" She smiled again "And the name's Jess." She added before heading for the kitchen.

"Well, that's mighty kind of you...Jess."
He looked around again and smiled as he met Mia's eyes glaring at him over the pages of her book, Max and Dustin's grinning faces, apart from the colour of their skin they looked identical, they must have spent so much time together that their mannerisms rubbed off on each other. Sheriff smiled, he thought they looked like a pair of novelty bookends. Then his gaze met Quack's again and they smiled at each other.

"Yeah, I'm Sheriff Russell... Dawn...Ms Rougeau told me that you folks were going to be staying up here and with it being winter and all, I just wanted to make sure you were all okay."

"Yeah, everything's just fine!" Quack said.

"Good, good! Is it just you five staying here?" He enquired.

"No, there's Sophie. She's asleep upstairs. And there's... Rob, but we don't know where he is." Quack shrugged.

"What, you mean he's missing?" Sheriff Russell enquired worryingly.

"Oh no, nothing like that, Sheriff!" Mia said, shaking her head.

"Then what do you mean?"

"Rob is Sophie's boyfriend, they had a fight and he stormed out." Mia added.

"I see!" Sheriff Russell nodded, he rubbed at his behind that was now on fire from the heat. From one extreme to another he thought and moved away from the fireplace.

"He's probably just gone for a smoke." Dustin added "To cool off."

"Well, he's in the right place for it out there!" chuckled The Sheriff, the others joined him in finding the irony in his little quip.

Jessica approached from the kitchen with a small thermos, that would carry no more than two cups worth of cocoa and handed it to him "There you go, Sheriff!" she said smiling "That should keep you warm out there."

He dreaded going back out there and repeating the trek back the other way, but it was the shadows that moved behind the trees that he dreaded most, not the snow, not the cold.

"Thank you!" He said taking it and placing his hat back on his head "I've taken up enough of your time, I'll bid you all goodnight."

"Goodnight, Sheriff!" came the almost orchestrated reply as Jessica walked him to the door.

"Now, you probably won't be able to get down to town for a

few days, as there is more snow on the way tomorrow. Well, not in your van anyway. By foot it may take you three hours. If I was you, I'd just stay in."

There was mass of heads nodding up and down in unison before him.

"You have enough food, yes?"

"Oh, yes, Sheriff! We're all good." Jessica added.

"Good!" He opened the door and the cold hit him again and that thought of those shadows dancing from tree to tree were there again. "You have my number I take it, if there are any problems?"

"Yes, Sir! Ms Rougeau has kindly jotted down several emergency numbers for us. Just in case."

"Good...Well, thanks for the cocoa. Stay safe."

Again several goodnights rang in the air as he walked out the door before stopping and swivelling on the spot.

"Oh! This other guy... Rob? Is he a big guy?"

They nodded.

"Yeah, he's a footballer." Mia said.

He looked out at the footprints, very large, exceedingly large, something didn't feel quite right about it. He looked back up at them "That would explain these big footprints then." He laughed "Some plates on that kid, huh?"

They laughed and he left still not feeling right about those footprints. The door closed and he was out in the cold and dark once more, he shivered and followed his own tracks back from where he came.

"Feet that size, kid's got to be at least 6, 5." He said to himself as he trudged back towards his truck that was an hour's trek away.

The cold wind nipped at his exposed chapped cheeks and the shadows played games again with his eyes. He took a sip of hot cocoa, it helped, but only a little.

CHAPTER 15

A beam of light slices through the gap in the thin linen curtains and cuts across Mia's sleeping face. She stirs and begins to stretch her limbs out under the thick comfortable duvet. Jessica spent the night downstairs on the sofa as the epic game of *Dungeons and Dragons* went on into the early hours. This allowed Mia to have a really good nights sleep and the luxury of the whole bed to herself. Her eyes opened and are immediately forced to close again, squinting tightly against the unrelenting sun. She groaned with annoyance and reached out blindly for her glasses that were perched on top of her book next to her cellphone. A tattered bookmark hung from the book like the tongue of a thirsty dog. She was more than halfway through now and excited to see where the story would go.

Grabbing her glasses she put them on and held out her hand in front of the light, trying to shield her tender eyes from it's ferocity, already she could see orbs of light everywhere as if she were dizzy, they were still there when she closed her eyes, in vibrant red behind her eyelids.

"That Goddamn sun!" She moaned, grabbing her cell phone and checking the time, 9:32 am stared back at her in bold white against the wallpaper of some large barbarian that clutched a broadsword in his hands, his ripped physique draped in fur. The battery was at 29%, she'd have to charge it up she thought and still there was no bars on her signal.

Can't expect good wireless connection in the middle of the woods.

She turned over away from the window and screamed. It was a short scream, formed from the startling sight of a deer's antlers protruding out from the covers, its head resting on the pillow next to her in the double bed.

"Those idiots!" She growled, clutching the palm of her hand to her chest. "I'll get those turds for this!" She added, obviously already assuming that Max and Dustin were to be held responsible for this particular prank.

She pulled back the duvet cover and her eyes grew like saucers and she screamed, this time the scream was out of sheer terror.

The colour drained from her cheeks at the sight of the mass amount of blood that had soaked into the sheets. She cupped a hand over her mouth to prevent her from vomiting, and she did so want to vomit. She fell backwards off the bed taking the duvet with her, she stood slowly and it was then that she saw what lay before her in all its grim glory.

The deer's head from a fresh kill lay next to her, giblets of flesh hung from its throat where it had been hacked away from its body.

"Oh, my god!" She murmured, she was now in total and utter shock.

The cold glazed eye of the deer shimmered in the sunlight and looked like it was winking at her, it's mouth hung slightly open and its pink podgy tongue dangled out, moist and lustrous like a fresh piece of liver.

It wasn't until she glanced down and noticed that her ivory fleeced one piece was covered in the deers blood too, that she screamed again. The screams were constant, ear splitting with fear gurgling in her throat.

She heard the sound of rushing footsteps   pummelling the wooden staircase as tears seeped from under the lenses of her glasses and ran down her plump light brown cheeks.

She then vomited on the exposed floorboards before feeling faint and joining the second coming of last nights Quack n' Mac, her glasses breaking against her unconscious face as she hit the floor.

CHAPTER 16

While some people were waking up to discover severed animal heads next to them in their beds, Sheriff Russell was already finishing up his second mug of shit coffee. His face contorted with its unpleasant taste and with the back of his hand, he wiped away the excess build up of it, that had clung onto the greying whiskers of his moustache.

He fingered through the file containing the 'Blackfoot Attack' that involved Chuck Muchnick and Professor Cumberbatch. He shook his head, something from each man's witness statements just didn't match up.

Something just didn't ring true to him.

"Something's just not right about all of this." He said to himself and then he heard the enthusiastic morning pleasantries of Deputy Clegg and his ears pricked up, he swivelled around on his chair and rose, his middle aged joints creaked as much as the chair did and the sheer effort of getting out of the chair was accompanied by a groan.

"Really must exercise." He coughed, feeling very unfit.

He grabbed his coat and hat and left his office walking towards the reception area. His rubber souls of his clumpy all-weather boots made an annoying squeaking against the laminate tiled flooring, but the sound was soon lost under the neighing laughter of   one

Raymond Clegg.

"Good morning, Raymond!" Sheriff Russell said as he entered the reception area.

"Oh! Good morning to you Sheriff!" Snorted Deputy Clegg in reply, still reeling from the joke he had just told Lieutenant Adams. She too was giggling as she sat behind the desk, rolling a pen between her manicured fingers.

"Glad to see you're in high spirits this morning, Raymond." Said The Sheriff as he put on his hat.

"Always, Sheriff! You know me!" He grinned that goofy grin of his.

"I sure do!" He smiled back, sliding on his jacket.

"It's a glorious day out there this morning too, Sheriff!" Adams added smiling with touches of lipstick staining her pearly whites.

"It really is!" The Sheriff nodded in agreement "May even thaw some of that shit out!"

"I wouldn't get too carried away, Sheriff!" Adams said shaking her head "We've got another heap of it on the way tonight."

"Oh the joy!" Sheriff sang sarcastically.

Clegg took off his jacket and passed behind the reception desk looking to hang it up on his peg "You off somewhere, Sheriff?"

"Yes, we are!" He said rigorously grinding his zip up as Clegg looked at him slightly confused.

"We?"

"We're going to go and see Mister Muchnick."

"Oh... Well, I haven't had chance to speak to him, to arrange..."

"It's okay. We'll surprise him!" Sheriff smiled.

Clegg reluctantly smiled back, but it was forced and he looked nervous.

"Now, put your coat back on and we'll get moving."

Clegg started to fumble with his jacket as Sheriff headed for the exit.

"See you later, Tammy!" He said holding a hand up to her "Hold my calls, unless it's anything important, obviously."

"You got it, Sheriff!" She called as the door closed behind him.

Deputy Clegg's skin looked clammy as he frantically struggled to get his jacket back on and his Ushanka perched askew on his mop of dark hair.

"Are you okay, Raymond?" Adams asked, with worry in her tone, the way a mother would ask a child.

"Yeah! Yeah, sure! I'm fine." He stuttered as he scuttled after the Sheriff.

Lieutenant Adams didn't looked convinced. She thought he looked like someone that was hiding something, but she figured it wasn't her concern and with a shrug of her shoulders she went back to her computer screen.

The small carpark of the Sheriff's Office had been shovelled and cleared of snow to allow easy access for the trucks. Peaked hills formed a wall around the area which had so kindly and painstakingly been cleared by Sergeant Nathan Brown, Nate to his friends. He was a damn hard worker was Nate, he only worked part time for the Sheriff's Office as he was also a firefighter for the town. Well, he'd drawn the short straw that morning and had cleared it in just over two hours, Sheriff Russell rewarded him by sending him over to

Dawn's for a late breakfast, on Sheriff Russell's tab of course.

They walked towards the truck and Sheriff Russell opened up the drivers door and waited for Clegg to catch up.

"Are you okay, Raymond?" The Sheriff asked. But he already knew from his jittery behaviour that there was definitely something his Deputy was keeping from him. It was the same strange behaviour he had witnessed from him last night at Dawn's.

"Yeah, Sheriff! I'm fine." He forced a smile out again and wished he could mop up that guilty sweat that had formed in the creases of his forehead.

"Okay!" The Sheriff grinned and started to step inside the truck and stopped "Oh, Raymond, I have some jobs I want you to do for me today."

"Yeah, sure!" He nodded waiting to hear what his daily chores were to be.

"I want you to make sure the Bobcat is fuelled up, as it may well be needed. Especially if we're going to have more of this shit!" He said as he angrily slapped a pile of icy snow from the roof of his truck.

"Yeah, no problem!" Clegg nodded.

"Also, All vehicles will need to have their tyres chained, that needs doing as soon as possible! Brown and Church will be taking out the other two later on and they'll need to be ready."

"Okay. What about yours?"

"She'll have to wait until I get back from seeing Muchnick." Clegg nodded and walked around to the passengers side. The Sheriff watched him closely, he did trust Clegg and he was a great deputy and a really likeable guy, a little excitable and hyperactive at times,

114

but a good guy nonetheless. He did trust him but there was something he wasn't telling him here and it revolved around this Blackfoot myth.

"It's okay, Raymond. You can make a start on your jobs now. I'll go and see Muchnick on my own."

"Oh... Are you sure? I mean it's no bother I can..."

"No, it's okay. You have enough to do as it is." He smiled at him and Clegg smiled back. Clegg's teeth ground down on each other as he fought back the urge to scream the truth that remained hidden behind his pearly whites. A truth that he had longed to tell. But after there were several seconds of uncomfortable silence, he decided to say nothing.

He stood on the carpark watching as Sheriff Russell drove away. Sheriff used his mirrors to watch his deputy too. When Clegg thought he was out of sight he hurried away, but not towards the garage or the other vehicles, but towards town.

"You're going to see Dawn, aren't ya Raymond?" He said to himself as he drove away "I'll let you play your games, whatever it may be, because I have a feeling it's all gonna come out when I see Muchnick anyhow."

He smiled as he drove away, today was a good day because his dials hadn't been tampered with and Willie Nelson's horsey croak spluttered out of the trucks speakers.

CHAPTER 17

Sophie shuffled down the stairs, wiping the sleep from her eyes as the others gathered around Mia who was sat sobbing on the sofa. Mia was covered in a layer of dried blood and fresh vomit, which had now matted her fleece onesie.

"What's all the commotion?" Sophie yawned.

The other's looked up at her in shock, not quite able to comprehend how she had slept through the last thirty minutes of drama. All of them but Dustin who stood shuffling his wrestling cards in his hands, looking a little melancholy.

"You really slept through that?" Asked Quack.

"I heard a scream." Sophie shrugged as she reached the main room of the cabin.

Mia turned to face her and Sophie's jaw dropped and hung in awe.

"This was the commotion!" Mia scoffed pointing to her rapidly swelling left eye, that now resembled a purple balloon, one that was in the process of being filled with air.

"Oh my God, Mia!" She said running to her side "What the hell happened?"

She then noticed the blood and vomit "Oh shit! Is that blood?"

"Yes, and vomit!" Mia said finally putting a stop to her snivelling.

"Did you cut yourself or something? Did somebody do this to

you?" Sophie probed with obvious concern.

"Here, put this on your eye!" Jessica said handing her a bag of frozen peas wrapped in a towel.

"Thanks!" Mia said and placed the ice cold package over the one side of her face, the coldness was numbing to her swelling eye and her pounding head was grateful for it.

"I fainted and banged my head." She lifted up the remains of the twisted metal and glass that had once formed her glasses, but now resembled some modern art sculpture, the kind nobody understands.

"Broke my glasses when I fell." She sighed.

"Hey, it could have been worse!" Smiled Max.
Mia scowled at him through her one good eye.

"I know it was you!" She growled "Or you, Dust!" She snapped her head whipping in his direction.

"What did I do?" They both announced in unison, a look of authentic shock on their faces, Dustin's sad eyes lifting from his constant shuffling of cards.

"It's just the kind of practical joke you morons would pull!" She sighed, throwing her demolished glasses onto the coffee table.

"What have I missed here?" Sophie asked, a little confused "How is it their fault?" Her eyes flitting around her friends, hoping for a definitive answer.

"Now, c'mon!" Quack announced "Let's not make accusations. They already said they had nothing to do with it!"

"To do with what?" Sophie asked again, even more confused now, her own head starting to ache and if it carried on like this she too would need an ice pack.

"Yeah...Well!" Mia groaned, probably knowing deep down that neither of them could do something so callous "Who did it then, Quack?" She added.

"I'm damned if I know!" Quack answered shaking his head "But, I do know it wasn't anyone in this cabin. Nobody here would do such a thing. Joking or not!"

"Do what!" Sophie shouted finally.

"The reason Mia vomited and fainted...and is covered in blood, was that somebody put the severed head of a deer in her bed." Jessica calmly put Sophie out of her misery.

"Oh my God!" Sophie sat shaking her head "That must have been so traumatic for you Mia?"

"Yep!" Mia said sarcastically as she looked down at herself, smothered in all manner of bodily fluids, that had now started to dry and reek of unpleasantness.

"Well, who could have done this?" Sophie asked looking around at everyone, none of them wanting to make eye contact with her, because they could only think of one person that it could be. They all had the same name dancing around on their tongues, but none of them brave enough to set it free.

"Oh!" Sophie said finally after she realised who they had fingered for this heinous rib.

"Sophie, we..." Jessica began to speak but Sophie stood up in annoyance and defiance "I knew you'd think it was him! I knew it!" Everyone looked away embarrassed.

"Do you have any proof it was Rob? Do you?" She yelled at them all, but nobody answered "Yeah, I didn't think so! Just because you guys don't like him that's no excuse to go around accusing him of things! He may be a lot of things but he would never do anything like that!"

"Calm down, Soph!" Quack said laying a hand on her shoulder.

She brushed it off and shouted "No I will not calm down! You never wanted him here in the first place did you, Quack? You hate him don't you?"

"Hell yeah I do!" Quack fired back which stunned Sophie "Yeah, I do hate him! I hate the way he treats you. I hate how arrogant he is and thinks he's better than us, he's a 24 carat dick!"

"Well, say what you feel!" Sophie said tears starting to ripple across her eyelids.

"Look." Quack said with a sigh "This isn't a witch hunt and we're not blaming him. But when he's not here to defend himself, we..."

"What do you mean he's not here?" Sophie asked looking around "Where is he?"

"He stormed out last night. Don't you remember? We haven't seen him since."

"What?" Sophie yelled.

"We thought you knew he'd left?" Jessica added.

"Well, yeah, I mean I thought he'd just gone to get some fresh air and he'd come back! I didn't think he'd just leave."

"Told you. He's a jackass, Soph!" Quack said.

"Yeah, well you don't know him like I do!"

"Soph, he only wanted to have sex with you, why can't you see that?" Quack pleaded.

"What? Like you, you mean!" She seethed. Quack's face lit

up like the glowing light of a police car's cherry.

"I..." He tried to answer, but couldn't look at her out of embarrassment.

"Yeah, I thought so. I've seen the way you look at me, drooling all over yourself! It's pathetic!"

Quack stomped towards the kitchen area in embarrassment, finding it extremely difficult to hold back tears, the kind of tears you shed when you've just had your heart broken.

"That was unfair, Soph!" Jessica said shaking her head "You know how much he cares about you!" And with that Jessica hurried after him.

"Whatever!" Sophie hissed storming back upstairs.

"Wow! How did that suddenly become all about Sophie?" Mia asked herself dabbing the ice pack again on her throbbing face. She shook her head as she stood up and slowly made her way upstairs.

Suddenly Dustin called out "Does nobody care that I've lost my limited edition Randy Rogan card?"

"No!" Max said unsympathetically, while giving him a hefty slap on the back.

"That bastard Rob! He lost it! I'm gonna kill him!" Dustin seethed in jest.

CHAPTER 18

Sheriff Russell sat on a weary decrepit armchair, its innards exploding out of several shredded areas in the threadbare upholstery. He gripped the heavily stained mug which had the words 'World's Greatest Lover' emblazoned on it, as he cringed at the contents (which was supposedly coffee, but Sheriff Russell had his reservations). It was black, thickened and had the texture of treacle. He decided he wouldn't be drinking it but he kept it sandwiched between his chapped hands as it was at least warming.

He looked around at the dirty old trailer that looked like it had never been cleaned, it probably hadn't he thought. It smelt of damp, urine and marijuana, not a pleasant combination.

"Smells like Goddamn fox piss in here!" He murmured to himself as his moustache danced the Cha Cha with his irritated twitching nostrils.

Moist and dirty cardboard boxes stood piled up against one wall of the trailer's living room, another corner saw years upon years of local newspapers tied together with frayed pieces of string. Then there were magazines, crumpled and damp most of them, the pages now most likely stuck together and really of no use to anyone now. In a way he thought that this was probably Charles Muchnick's filing system, I guess it worked for him.

He heard Muchnick clunking around in the John while he waited patiently for him.

"Is everything all right in there, Mr Muchnick?" The Sheriff called.

"Fine." Came a muffled response.

"Probably trying to get rid of your stash aren't ya, Chuck." He chuckled to himself and for a second, had a momentary lapse and almost succumbed to taking a swig of that foul bubbling mug of mud he held in his grasp.

"I'll be out in a minute, Sheriff!" Came the gurgled cry from the toilet.

"Don't rush on my account." Sheriff hollered back, with just the hint of sarcasm.

He stood up and took a wander around the trailer, it was in such a state that it was almost as if someone had just up and left it and not been back to it for years, leaving it to rot and fester. He looked at photographs that hung on the wall, some had framed articles from the local newspapers about Blackfoot sightings. Some were family photographs, one with his father holding a gigantic Walleye, both of them beaming with pride, while little Charles Muchnick (who was around nine in the picture) held onto the fishing rods. The greyscale pictures had started to become sepia in its colouring due to excess cigarette smoke. One picture intrigued Sheriff Russell and he leaned in for a closer look. The photograph was of several men clad in hunting garbs, hands clutching their chosen rifles as they stood over the gigantic carcass of a grizzly bear. As he investigated the photograph he noticed some familiar faces. Charles Muchnick was there of course (He looked a lot younger), The currently missing hunter, Elroy Pascoe, as well as his predecessor, Keith W.

Windwood. Then there was Bruce Hardwood (Chopper to his friends) who was the owner of the only bar in town 'Choppers', there was Drew Cartwright, 'Old Sparky' Jeff Thurman and a huge bearded mountain of a man that he hadn't seen before. On the lower righthand corner, the year 1997 was scribbled on it.

The toilet flushed, its vibrations shaking the loose panelled structure that sat out in the middle of nowhere away from anyone and everyone. Charles Muchnick waddled out of the bathroom with a flurry of gravelly coughs while hitching up stained disheveled trousers. A face of stubble framed that infamous gummy smile of his and his hair (what was left of it) was in disarray like he'd been dragged through a hedge.

"Sorry about that, Sheriff! Nature called, and you gotta answer those calls in't ya?" He cackled as he shuffled liked a penguin suffering from a severe case of haemorrhoids across the living room, before collapsing unceremoniously into his surprisingly newish looking lazy-boy recliner.

"Take the weight off, Sheriff." He said as he pulled the leaver on the side launching his legs up into a more comfortable position. The Sheriff sat down and found himself looking at his lazy-boy, and wondering how he missed it. It didn't go with the rest of the festering decor.

"I see you're admiring my chair!"

"It's a nice chair, Mr Muchnick." The Sheriff replied with a nod of his head.

"Hell of a nice chair! You can thank your deputy for it!" He grinned, rubbing his hands over the soft arm rests.

"Really? Deputy Clegg got you that?"

"He sure did. I didn't really have anything when I moved in here. Only thing I had to sit on was that piece of shit you're on!" He laughed "But seriously, Raymond is a good kid. He's really looked after me, since...well since I moved in here."

"He sure has!"

"So, what is it that I can do for ya, Sheriff? I'm always open to helping the brave men and women that allow us to sleep safely in our beds at night." He grinned, again those few teeth he had stuck out like tusks.

"I wanna talk about Blackfoot."

"Oh! Do you now?" His wide eyes twinkled with passion, a burning desire that you could almost feel, "My favourite subject! I warn you though, I could literally talk your damn ears off about yetis."

"It's The Blackfoot in particular I'm interested in."

"Okay." He answered, nodding with intrigue "What d'you wanna know?"

"It's one incident in particular I'd like to know about. The incident where you and Professor Cumberbatch were supposedly attacked by it."

The fire died in his eyes and it was replaced by fear, you could see it manifest in his face with just the mention of Cumberbatch's name and a far away stab of reminiscence was triggered. He swallowed hard and picked up a can of Bobby's light that was sitting on a small table, which was held together by grey electrical tape. He sipped the beer and then gurgled "I can't really remember that far back, it's all a blur now."

He didn't look at The Sheriff, he couldn't bring himself to make eye contact.

"C'mon, I'm sure you can remember something about that day?"

He took another swig of beer and shook his head "Not really."

"Well, what do you remember about it?" The Sheriff continued to probe.

"I gave my statement to Sheriff Windwood and it was good enough for him!" He snapped.

"I'm just following up on some new information that's all."

"What new information?" He snapped again, his head jerking to face The Sheriff, his saucer like eyeballs looking like they could fall from their sockets at any moment and roll around the floor of the trailer.

"I've been looking through the file and your statement and the Professor's statement don't really tally up."

"Why's that? We both saw the same thing!"

"Well, you are on record as stating it was indeed the illusive Blackfoot creature. But Cumberbatch said..." The Sheriff placed his mug down on the precarious table for a moment as he retrieved his notepad "Give me a second..." He apologised as he flicked through the pages "Ah, here we are! He is on record as saying, and I quote 'My vision was impaired and my head was woozy, but at first glance it appeared to me like it was a bear. It was as big as a bear but as I focussed, and I remember this because I was fixated on those stone cold eyes, which made me see things clearly for a few seconds and I saw a beard! I'm pretty damn sure it was the face of a man.'" He closed up the note pad and slid it back into his chest pocket.

"He said it himself he was knocked six ways to Sunday! How'd he know what he saw?" Muchnick scoffed.

"Where I come from, Bear's don't tend to have beards Mr Muchnick!"

There was a pause and for a moment the two stared at each other, like duelling chess masters locked in a stalemate.

"I ain't saying shit!" Muchnick finally spat before focussing on his beer again.

"Then I'll bid you a good morning, Mr Muchnick." He said standing up appearing to leave, then stood next to Muchnick and slapped the can of beer out of his hand, the contents fizzed and bubbled as it erupted from the can and landed on the floor, soiling the already gruesome looking carpet.

"Enough of the fucking bullshit!" The Sheriff yelled, screaming into Muchnick's frightened face. "I know there is something going on around here, I'm not completely stupid! Everyone's been on tenterhooks since the snow started to fall. Now you either tell me what happened that night or I take you in on possession of Marijuana with intent to distribute!"

"But, I..." Muchnick stuttered.

"I know you've got a whole heap of that shit hidden away here!" He didn't know that of course, he was just surmising "May I remind you that it's still illegal to distribute Marijuana without a license."

"Okay, okay!" The words shook out of him matching his nerves that were now shot. Sheriff Russell had put the frighteners on him so much that he would have told him the size of his dick if he'd have asked him. Luckily for his pride that wasn't the information

126

that he wanted.

Sheriff Russell calmed himself and sat back down in the chair.

Muchnick took a deep breathe "It wasn't a Blackfoot that attacked us, it wasn't a bear or any other creature...It was a man!"

"Who was this man?"

"His name... his name is Tooth. Beau Tooth!"

"Beau Tooth?"

"Oh, Fuck it!" Muchnick grizzled and burst into tears "I've really let the cat out now! Oh pisser!"

"Calm down and just tell me who this guy is?"

Muchnick howled with hysterical cries, years of pent up fear, anxiety and guilt was flushing out of his system. In truth I guess he'd always wanted to tell someone.

"Who is he?"

"He is a killer!" He sniffed "He's murdered people, lots of people! We've sat back as a community and done nothing year after year." He began to cry again.

"Is he still out there in the woods?"

Muchnick didn't answer he just sobbed into his hands.

"Do you know where?"

Muchnick didn't reply again, he just went on crying his guilty little heart out.

Sheriff Russell couldn't take anymore and leaning over in his chair he paint brushed Muchnick across his face with a vicious right palm.

"Tell me, Goddamn it!" The Sheriff yelled.

Muchnick looked up at him with despair in his eyes, like a ex Vietnam veteran relieving an unpleasant flashback that still haunted him.

"I need to know, Muchnick! I have a whole town of people at risk here!"

"I don't know if he's still out there. I just don't know. Every year I pray to God that he's not, but I just don't know. But if he is, you'll never find him. I've looked for what was out there and when I found it... I nearly died!"

"Who else knows about this?" Sheriff asked.

But all Muchnick's blubbering had brought on a fit of coughing so he had to excuse himself. He scuttled off towards the bedroom and Sheriff Russell rubbed a hand across his moustache deep in thought. He quickly retrieved his notepad again and scribbled down the name Beau Tooth in his ineligible penmanship.

"Beau Tooth?" He murmured, his forehead creasing as he tried to process the name through his memory banks but kept coming up short.

There was the deafening wail of a Fitz Colt snub nose and then the horror that haunted the deranged mind of Charles Muchnick was finally over, as grey matter disturbingly splattered the wall of his bedroom.

CHAPTER 19

The lunch time rush had passed and Dawn Rougeau could finally breathe and get the chance to have her own lunch. Sparky had just left as always, he ate all his meals at Dawn's, every single day. Dawn thought that the old codger must really be giving his pension a hammering eating out everyday, not that he ate a lot, he was more there for the company.

Finally she was alone and sat down on one of the stools unwrapping a homemade BLT, she licked her lips with the anticipation and her stomach gurgling eagerly. She picked one half of it up, her rough workers fingers forcing several indents into the soft white slices. She took a bite, a big one and closed her eyes in ecstasy.

"So good!" She groaned, as the lettuce crunched sharply in her mouth.

The phone rang, she sighed with annoyance and at first was going to let it ring out, but its bothersome whining ate away at her and she relented.

"Always when I sit my ass down to eat! Always!" She growled slamming the sandwich down on top of the other half, causing the juice from the freshly sliced tomatoes to ooze out onto the untouched half, causing it to soak into the bread, causing a vulgar discolouration.

"Hello?" She snapped yanking up the receiver before

immediately composing herself and becoming a bit more professional "Dawn's, how can I help ya?"

"Hi, Ms Rougeau!" came the soft reply.

"Who is this?"

"It's Jess!"

There was a long pause and neither of them spoke, the cogs turning rapidly in Dawn's head. Did she even know a Jess?

"Jessica Head?" The voice spoke again "I'm at the cabin?"

"Oh! Of course!" Dawn remembered "Is everything okay, my dear?"

Jessica laughed a little at the 'dear' part of her question, the irony was not lost on her.

"There's been an... erm..." Jess searched for the correct word "... an incident?"

"What kind of incident?" Dawn asked, nervously.

"One of the girls found the head of dead deer in her bed this morning!"

Dawn didn't say anything, but cupped a hand around her mouth, her eyes widening.

"Hello? Ms Rougeau..." Jess said.

But still there was no reply. Dawn found herself gazing off and looking at the Maple Falls memories that smothered the far wall of the diner.

"Hello? Are you there?" Jess asked again.

"I..." Dawn answered and then said nothing as she remained focusing on the framed photographs, her gaze closing in on one memory in particular.

"Ms Rougeau?" Came the call from the other end of the

130

receiver again.

"There's... really... bad line..." Dawn lied.

"Can you hear me?" Jess called again.

"I... Hello?..." Dawn pretended as tears filled her eyes. Tears of guilt.

Jess continued trying to get through, but still Dawn didn't answer. Her moist eyes drawn to the hunters that were gathered around the massive bulk of a dead Grizzly. A huge beast that was given the name 'Bigelow' which had been stuffed years ago and now resided over at Chopper's bar.

"Can you hear me, Hello? Hello?" Jess frantically called.

"Line..." She paused dramatically "...really...bad..." Tears trickled down her face now and dripped onto her name badge, her full attention focussed on the hunters.

"What shall we do?" Jess tried again.

Dawn's moist eyes panned along to the largest man on the photograph.

"Should we be worried?" She asked again. "There's blood everywhere. It's ruined the sheets!"

She stared at the bearded man that grinned back at her.

"Tooth!" Dawn whispered.

"Sorry?" Jess replied "I can't hear you! Is it the line?"

Dawn's mouth wobbled and her ageing pursed lips wrinkled, cutting lines into her *Ruby Red* brand lipstick. She mouthed the words 'I'm sorry' but those words would not come.

She could still hear Jess speaking when she hung up the receiver and stood for a moment tears streaking in lines of black mascara as she stared at the picture on the wall. It was as if there was no longer any photographs on the wall at all, just that one, zooming in on one face in particular, that of Beau Tooth.

There was silence and then the phone rang again, Dawn screamed at the top of her lungs, a hysterical shriek and grabbed the telephone that was stuck to the wall and ripped it away. Plaster burst from the wall, some of it clung to the base of the phone the rest crumbled to the checkerboard tiles. She screamed and yanked again, tearing the wire out of its socket, bringing with it yet more wall and plaster. She cradled the whole thing in her arms like a baby as tears dripped onto it. She gazed down at it and then let go, allowing the whole thing to just come crashing down to the floor.

She fell to her knees, her white stockings tearing with the impact and she sobbed into her hands.

"It's starting again!" She weeped "Oh God, please forgive me!" She cried.

She sobbed for what seemed like five minutes and then the thought came to her that what if someone walked in now? What would they think? She looked up, her face smeared with make up and tears. She sniffed and inhaled the seeping mucus that was escaping from her nostrils. Her eyebrows withered with a look of guilt ridden remorse and she screamed again. She glanced at the picture one last time before rising up and hurtling towards the wall of memories and grabbing the photograph from the wall.

"Goddamn you Beau Tooth! God fucking damn you!" She cried and threw the frame to the floor. It exploded like a firework display of glass and wood, as the photograph sat harmlessly on a bed of glass staring up at her, judging her.

She collapsed into a booth seat and with her head in her hands again, she cried.

"What have I done?" She asked herself, knowing that the tears she shed could never wash away the remorse she would feel for the rest of her days.

CHAPTER 20

Quack slipped on his large thick beige coloured Parker, that had been sitting on top of the pile of other jackets on the sofa.

Sophie had yet to return and rejoin the others after the fight earlier, an altercation that had left Quack very upset. Mia was sitting in what was quickly becoming her favourite armchair as she battled to read her book through one cracked lens of her mangled spectacles.

Max and Dustin were on their hands and knees, still scouring for his missing wrestling card.

Quack slumped down onto the sofa and started to slip on his all-weather boots.

"Still not found that card?" He asked the two crawling explorers.

"No!" Snapped Dustin, his head lost under a bear skin rug that lay in front of the fireplace.

"I still think Rob took it!" Max added, peaking out from behind the sofa causing Quack to jump.

"Now, why the hell would he take that?" Quack asked shaking his head, as he struggled to tie his boot laces over his rotund stomach.

"Spite!" Dustin called from under the sweltering heat of the bearskin.

"More likely he did a quick EarlBAY scan and found out

what it's actually worth!" Max added lolling on the back of the sofa.

"Why? What's it worth?" Quack asked, stopping his lace tying in a moment of intrigue.

"Only around 42 bucks!" Max said enthusiastically.

"Is that all!" Quack scoffed rolling his eyes and sliding on his other boot.

"Is that all!" Calls Max in disbelief.

"Will you guys keep it down!" Mia pleaded "It's hard enough trying to read this with one eye and through a cracked lens without you goofballs hollering!"

"Sorry, Mia." Quack replied.

There was a moment of silence and Max disappeared behind the sofa again.

Jessica hurried down the stairs and noticed Quack was getting ready to head out "Hey Big man, Where ya going?" She asked.

"I thought I'd go and see if Rob was still out there somewhere." Quack answered.

"How nice of you!" She beamed.

"You really think he's still out there?" Mia asked.

"I don't know!" Quack shrugged standing and zipping his jacket up "Maybe he stopped the night in the van? Or maybe he made his way to town, surely we should see his tracks at least."

"Maybe the asshole froze to death!" came Max's retort from behind the sofa.

"Well, we need to know one way or another!" Quack announced, planting a jolly hat on over his mass of curly dark hair and yanking it down to cover his ears.

"I'll come with you!" Jessica said smiling and joined him at the sofa digging out her red Parker, which was easy to find with its hood and cuffs trimmed with mousey coloured fur.

"Cool!" Quack smiled back "The more the merrier!"
She grabbed her jacket and slipped it on and then hurried over to retrieve her fur topped boots that sat by the door. She brought them back to where Quack was standing and placed them on the floor in front of her, she smiled at Quack and he looked back in amazement, that hypnotising sparkle in her eyes, why had he never noticed that before?
She grabbed onto his broad shoulder and used him as a crutch as she stood on one leg and attempted to slip her foot into her boot, that was dressed in an excessively thick sock.

Dustin backed out from underneath the bear skin, his face clammy with sweat.

"He wouldn't have known how much it was worth!" He cries panting and getting his breath back.
Everyone looked at him.

"There's no wifi in this place or hadn't anyone noticed? He couldn't check anything out here. Our cells are practically useless!" Dustin added standing up.
Jessica slipped on her other boot and zipped them both up and then looking at Quack she flung her hood up into place.

"Ready?"

"Ready!" Quack smiled.
The pair approached the door slipping on gloves and opening the cabin up to the chilling wind outside. Everyone shuddered.

"See you guys later." Jessica hollered and Quack held a hand up and waved.

"Please be careful out there!" Mia moaned "It'll be dark in a few hours and there is another heap of snow on its way!"

"And thank you Miss Chung for the weather forecast." Quack mocked.

Everyone laughed.

"Fine!" Mia scoffed turning her attentions back to her book "Freeze to death! See if I care!"

As they left closing the door behind them, Max jumps up from behind the sofa.

"Eureka!" He shouts.

"You found him?" Dustin cries running towards him almost slipping on the shiny floorboards.

"Yep! He was under the sofa!" Max says proudly, but his attention was seemingly fixated on something else that he had hidden out of sight behind the sofa.

"I love you Maximus!" Dustin said arriving in a whirlwind of excitement "Gimme, gimme, gimme!"

Max handed him the card still focusing on something else. Dustin was too interested in getting his hands back on Randy Rogan to realise that his partner in crime was brewing something up.

"Never leave me again!" He said to the 2 1/2 inches by 3 1/2 inches piece of card while kissing it several times "Promise me you never will?"

"You wanna see what else I've found?" Max smiled a mischievous grin.

"Sure!" Dustin said nonchalantly.

Mia's curiosity had also been pricked and she too was waiting to see what he'd found.

"It must have dropped out of Rob's pocket last night." Max said and held up a small bag containing three rolled up joints.

"Shit!" Dustin whispered.

"I know right!" Max neighed.

"No way you guys! No drugs!" Mia scoffed.

Max and Dustin looked at each other and grinned mirroring grins that would have made even the cheshire cat jealous.

Outside the sky had already started to become bombarded with angry looking clouds, barging into each other and preventing that splendid blue sky from earlier in the day to break through.

Quack and Jessica trudged over towards the van that was now covered in a topping of thick snow. Its wheels could no longer be seen and from a distance it looked like some futuristic vehicle from a science fiction film, hovering in the air.

"Was Sophie okay when you went to see her?" Quack asked, a cloud of vapour escaping his mouth as he spoke.

Jessica paused for a moment and thought *How many times have I got to give him the eye or the signals! But, yet still all he cares about is Sophie.*

But she didn't say any of that.

"Yeah, she apologised to me for her outburst."

"Oh! Right!" He scoffed "It's me she needs to apologise too!"

"Oh, I agree!" Jessica nodded, her large red hood bouncing up and down "But I think she's embarrassed, so you may have to wait a bit longer for your apology."

Neither of them said anything else as they arrived at the van. Quack wiped at the window, trying to scrape away the ice that had built up on the glass. Finally he did and he peered inside.

"He's not in there." Quack said, his breath immediately attacking the glass and causing it to fog up.

They gazed around and looked back down the long drive that they drove up only yesterday. It was covered in a perfect blanket of white.

"There are no footprints towards the town!" Jessica said gazing around the entire area "No footprints anywhere!"

"We must have had more snow fall last night than we thought. It's covered up all the tracks."

"He must have gone to town, right?" Jessica asked.

"I hope so!" Quack shrugged "Where else could he be?"

Their eyes met again and the brightness of the fallen snow seamed to create a celestial halo around her, his loins tingled and for the first time he felt the urge to kiss her. Her eyelids seemed to dance playfully luring him to do so. But he didn't. He could not take the rejection from the two women in his life he deeply cared for.

"Shall we go for a walk?" He finally asked.

"Yeah, why not!" Jessica replied and the two trudged off towards Old Syrup.

CHAPTER 21

Sheriff Russell sat at the end of the sticky bar in Chopper's, an empty whiskey glass trembling in his jittering hands, as he stared into the bottom of the glass.

He didn't hear the gossip already being passed from lips to ear around the bar. He didn't hear the proprietor, Bruce 'Chopper' Hardwood ask if he'd like another, and he didn't even hear his favourite Skynyrd song, *Freebird* blaring from the jukebox.

His mind was elsewhere, his mind was replaying the days events out for him on a relentless loop, without the capability to pause or stop it. Unfortunately it just kept on playing out again and again in his minds eye.

One minute he's gazing into that thick dark muck that had allegedly been conceived from a coffee bean, waiting for Charles Muchnick to return, while he sat on an old deformed piece of shit that may have once resembled an armchair, springs uncomfortably using is ass as a pin cushion.

But Charles Muchnick never did return. Never did say another word on this Beau Tooth character, or anything else for that matter, and he never would again either.

The gunshot shook the trailer and shook him, he remembered bolting out of the chair and knocking over the coffee table that was being held together by a mass of electrical tape, it hit the floor but he heard nothing, just the reverberating of the gunshot all around him. The mug fell to the floor and out vomited the black substance, seeping out like some great oil slick, consuming the worn threadbare carpet.

"Another one sheriff?"

The first thing he saw was the wall doused in blood and brain with tiny fragments of his skull mixed in.

"Patrick?"

The suicidal concoction slowly trickled down the wall where his body lay. His face unrecognisable now, even to his own mother.

"Are you okay, Sheriff?"

A hole in his face so big it could have been dug by a woodchuck. The Sheriff suddenly guffawed as he imagined the head of a bloodstained woodchuck poking out of the crater that had been left in his face.

"Are you okay?" Came the distant voice.

Sheriff Russell blinked and he was back in the bar, back in Chopper's, he looked around and heard *Freebird* working its way around the lounge, eyes all watching him and whispering, passing on their gossip to each other. He saw the gargantuan bear, Bigelow proudly stuffed and mounted and standing in the corner of the bar without a care in the world. Next to it hung on dark wooden wall panelling, the photograph of the great white hunters.

"You sure you're okay, Patrick? Can I get you another drink?" Came the gravelly, but soothing voice of Chopper.

"Chopper?" Managed to leave The Sheriff's lips as he tried to focus on this confused wrinkled face that appeared before him, that was wearing a concerned look.

"Yeah, it's me!" He said placing a hand over the quivering

141

glass that The Sheriff had been gripping so tight that Chopper thought he might actually break it.

The shaking stopped and The Sheriff finally focussed.

"Chopper... I'm so sorry, I was miles..."

"Miles away?" Chopper chuckled "My reckoning is you were on the Isle of Dikaku!"

"Yeah!" Sheriff Russell laughed.

"I heard about Chuck." Chopper sighed shaking his head "Terrible business that."

"Yeah! Try being there!"

"I think I'll get you another drink. You look as though you need it!"

"Thanks!"

"You on duty?" Chopper asked turning to the array of spirts hanging together behind the bar, and pressed out a generous helping of Hackenschmidt Whiskey into the glass.

"Fuck it!" Sheriff Russell said and took the glass, his hand still a little shaky.

"You just make sure you take it easy. Witnessing that sort of shit can mess with a man's psyche."

"It sure fucking does!" Sheriff Russell nodded in agreement and had a sip of his drink.

There was a moment of silence and *Freebird* came to an end, the bar was as quiet as it was going to get, just the mumbles of conversations could be heard. Chopper was about to move on and go about his chores when Sheriff Russell looked up from his whiskey. It must have been some look because it immediately halted Chopper

"Can I ask you something Bruce?" Asked Sheriff Russell.

Chopper's thick wispy eyebrows rose and flickered, he knew what ever came next was serious. Nobody called him Bruce unless it was serious.

"Shoot!" Chopper said, leaning on the bar with curiosity stamped on his weathered face.

Sheriff Russell looked around the bar first, to see if anyone was earwigging. Just as the next 45 was randomly shuffled into place, sitting nicely on the turntable and after a second or two of static, and then the twang of an acoustic chord struck and the gruff gnarling of *Johnny Cash* singing '*Hurt*' crept out of the speakers hauntingly.

"Can you tell me about..." The Sheriff said before stopping himself and just making sure that nobody was listening "...Beau Tooth" The name seeped through the narrow gaps in his teeth and came out like the hiss of a snake, a whisper. But Chopper heard it, he heard the name all right. There was a flicker of an eyelid, almost like a nervous twitch that gave it away. Chopper said nothing in reply, but wiped his hands on the towel that was draped over his shoulder, and then let the towel fall onto the bar, that was sticky and moist and filled with dozens of watermarks left imprinted by beer glasses of the past.

Chopper turned to his wife who was at the other side of the bar, leant over having a conversation with a regular.

"Wendy?" He hollered, interrupting *Johnny Cash* in mid sentence.

"Yeah?" She replied.

"I'm going out back!" He replied, lifting up the section of bar and ushering The Sheriff through with a flick of his head.

Wendy looked back at him and nodded a solemn look on her face as she knew what was about to be discussed.

"C'mon, Sheriff! Bring your drink."

Sheriff Russell slunk from down from his stool on the other side of the bar and stepped into the unknown. Well, unknown to the customers anyway.

Sheriff Russell found himself in a small room, that doubled as a storage area and as Chopper's den. There was a card table, the remains of a forgotten game of solitaire abandoned on a bed of soft emerald felt. There were two armchairs sat next to a stove heater that was on and giving out some real heat. Chopper offered Sheriff Russell a seat and he sat, sinking down into the soft comfortable armchair. As Chopper prodded around the glowing embers with a poker, he looked around and admired the animal heads attached to the walls like novelty wall hooks. He kept expecting to see a jacket or a hat hung on a deers antlers. Chopper then walked over to the corner of the room where several boxes stood stacked, Hackenschmidt Whiskey stamped on some, Volkoff Vodka on some others and Queen Sherry on another. He delved into the box and retrieved a brand new bottle of whiskey, he expertly whipped the top off of the bottle and it spun into the air before falling to the wooden floorboards below. He sunk down into the chair opposite and took a deep swig.

"So, you wanna know about Beau Tooth, huh?" He asked.

"I'd like someone to fill me in, yeah!"

Chopper laughed "I guess people have been a bit cagey since the snow startled to fall again, haven't they?"

"They sure have!" Nodded The Sheriff taking another sip.

"I guess its Maple Falls best kept secret. I reckon all the

small towns over North America have them."

"You could be right, Chopper."

Chopper's smile soon disappeared as he stared at the dancing flames in the stove as if they were reaching to get out. Chopper looked away as if he wanted to climb inside and join the flames. He became mesmerised by the fire, it was obvious that he was conjuring up old memories that he had tried to ignore and leave behind. But there they were being played out again in front of his very eyes.

"Beau Tooth was one of the boys. Big son of a bitch, huge! And as strong as a bison I can tell ya!"

Chopper's face was actually grinning when he started his tale, I guess he was remembering the good side of Beau Tooth, before things changed.

"He was a lumberjack, lived out in one of the cabins in Maple Woods. Had a beautiful wife, Marcy and two sweet little girls... Abigail and Charlotte... They were darling little treasures!" His eyes saddened as he continued to look into the sweltering stove, remembering the distorted faces of the past as they seem too flutter in the amber glow.

"Those beautiful little girls!" His bottom lip began to flounder and Sheriff Russell thought that he could see a moist glaze shimmering on his eyes. But he coughed and cleared his throat, surpassing any emotion deep down into his gut.

"Yeah, he worked as a lumberjack, good one, very successful, always made his quota and got his shit together, you know?"

The Sheriff nodded.

"He was part of our happy band! The Bear Busters!" He

laughed and then stopped "You know old Bigelow in the bar?"
Sheriff Russell nodded.

"We got him back in '97. Man, what a heavy son of a whore he was!" He chuckled shaking his head "Biggest Grizzly I've ever seen!"
He took another big swig and washed the whiskey around his teeth.

"There was a bunch of us that used to meet up and hunt together... I have a photograph somewhere around here..." He started to rise but The Sheriff interrupted him "It's okay. I've already seen it. Muchnick had a copy."

"Yeah, of course he did!" Chopper said sitting back down.

"Yeah, there was me, obviously. Chuck, Goddamn loony always going on about that damn Blackfoot!" He shook his head and laughed.

"Is there a Blackfoot out there? Some kind of beast or creature?" The Sheriff interrupted.

"If there is, I never saw one." Chopper shrugged "But, Chuck swore blind that he'd seen it! He believed it was out there somewhere." He shook his head and gazed back into the fire.

"Old Sparky was also one of the gang, and then there was Drew Cartwright, Elroy Pascoe and our fearless leader, Keith W, your predecessor." He looked at him and they both nodded and sipped at the same time.

"Hell of a man he was!" Chopper sighed.

"You talk about him as if he's dead?" Said The Sheriff looking a little bemused.
Chopper turned again to face him and their eyes met, with the golden reflection of the fire in his eyes the intensity was real.

"He is dead!" Chopper whispered his bottom lip trembling.

"What?" Sheriff Russell gasped, his green eyes like saucers "What do you mean he's dead? How? You must come to the office right now and make a statement! I..."

"Just listen will ya!" Chopper snapped and that was enough to know that there was yet more to come from Chopper Hardwood.

CHAPTER 22

Twilight had waved its magic wand across the sky, replacing the harsh greys with a pallet of vanilla and pink that merged together like lovers, and the dying sun added the finishing touches to an unmatchable picturesque masterpiece that produced a wonderful presentation of glowing coral clouds.

"Doesn't the sky look beautiful?" Gasped Jessica as they stood at the edge of the frozen lake.

"It really does!" Replied Quack, not really looking at the sky, but at Jessica who's sweet glowing face peeped out from under her enormous hood.

"I'd make the most of it though. Those clouds mark trouble." He sighed.

"Pink sky at night..." Jessica started to say when Quack swallowed hard and reached out to hold her hand. Jessica turned to look at him, he was now focussed on the beautiful sky, he dared not face her incase she didn't appreciate his advances. He could no longer take anymore rejection.

She looked down at their gloved hands cupped together like a yin and yang symbol and a smile caressed her lips, blood immediately filling her cold cheeks as she blushed.

"Quack?" She said softly.

His heart skipped a beat and an anxious layer of sweat immediately built up underneath his woolly hat, then slowly started to trickle down his temples.

Oh shit! Oh God! Oh fuck! She's gonna pull away isn't she? I read the signals wrong didn't I? You're an idiot Chester! An ass to think that...

"Quack?" She asked again and this time he was forced out of his nervous reverie.

"Yeah?" he answered facing her and swallowing hard again as his doughy dark eyes met hers for the first time ever.

Have you ever really looked into someones eyes? The window to the soul that will tell you more than words could ever say.

He was amazed at how beautiful they appeared to him, the colour of ferns, sprinkled with lavender toned flecks throughout her iris'.

"Will you kiss me?" She asked, the words wavering as they left her lips. She too was obviously apprehensive that he would even want to.

He swallowed again, deeply, so deep that they both heard it. He thought it was so loud that it echoed several times around the frozen Old Syrup that lay before them.

"I've never... I mean... I..." He stuttered, face clammy, heart beating, a flutter of excitement in his loins.

"It's okay." She smiled, so very softly and inviting, the kind of smile you need when you're feeling down. It was that special type of smile that tells you everything is going to be okay. Quack needed this in his life.

They both leant in and closed their eyes. Unfortunately they both banged heads, a sound loud and dazzling, like two beer glasses meeting in a toast. They both pulled back in unison with matching yelps. Then rubbing their heads, they both burst into laughter. They had shared many a moment like that just laughing at each other, as friends, but now that humour quelled the seriousness of the situation, and was calming. Their eyes met again and the laughter stopped.

"Shall we try again?" She asked and Quack nodded.

"Let's keep our eyes open this time." She giggled.

And they did. Their lips met and they moved in closer, holding each other, their eyes closed as they fell into each other in such a perfectly beautiful moment.

Not far away, childlike howls whisked around cabin number three. Laughter echoed through the snow covered trees as Max, Dustin and Mia took part in a playful snowball fight. Mia had finally let her hair down and joined them in some frolics. She may have told you that it was because she couldn't focus on her book properly to read through her broken glasses, its lens now resembling a kaleidoscope. If she told you that, it would be a lie. The joint that they had all smoked about an hour ago may have had something to do with the loss of her inhibitions.

Sophie watched them from the bathroom window, her pretty face scrunched up and grouchy. The rapid noise of the bath filling drowned out some of the gleeful merriment that she was missing out on, and the hot mist filled the room and smothered the window in condensation, which gave her the perfect veil to hide behind.

"Fine! Have your fun and games!" She sulked "Nobody cares about me."

She sighed, feeling sorry for herself and beginning to reflect the demeanours of her newer friends she had met at college since dating Rob, the popular arrogant ones that think they own the place.

The bathtub was almost full and she turned off the taps, leaving several drips to fall into the warm inviting waters causing ripple after ripple. She caught her reflection in the bath water before it was distorted and she didn't care for it. She walked away towards the mirrored cabinet that was attached to the wall, wiping away the condensation with her hand, she stared at her face and she could not believe how miserable she appeared.

"What the hell am I doing?" She asked her reflection "This isn't me! It's not who I am. I think it's high time I realise that it's better to be who I really am than to try and be someone I'm not!"

She tied her long golden hair up into a loose bun and smiled.

"Those are my true friends down there and I've been a dick to them. I will have to change that, I'll have to apologise." She then remembered what she had said to Quack "I definitely owe Quack an apology."

She disrobed and shuddered, her exquisite young figure suddenly covered in a layer of gooseflesh as she quickly skipped naked towards the bath. Slowly she stepped in and her body quivered with the heat of the water.

"Hot, hot, hot!" She murmured as she sat down, allowing some time for her body to adjust to sudden change in temperature. The heat was comforting and when she was relaxed she allowed herself to slide down under the water. Her face and knees the only parts of her that could be seen above the water, like three misshapen desert islands waiting to be discovered. She could no longer hear anything with her ears submerged, and now the decision to sink underneath the water made the tying up of her hair a pointless exercise, it came loose and fluttered around under the water like a jellyfish.

She smiled, finally feeling like herself again and thought of the fun evening that lay in front of her, one of laughter, good food and good company. Obviously she would have to make her apologies first. The thought of saying sorry to everyone for being a jerk made her anxious and she could feel that chain of stress wrap around her chest and constrict. She felt for a moment that the stress may become too much, and she did what she always did in times of stress, she touched herself. She had obviously done it lots of times now and she knew where she liked to be touched and what worked, it always managed to take that stressful feeling away and replace it with a pleasant one. Her hand wriggled through the water like and eel and settled on her thigh which she caressed with her pruning fingers gently tickling the inside of her thigh. She then rubbed gently at her fleshy labia, the pleasurable caress was accompanied by a sigh and she could already feel the links in that chain of stress slacken. She used all of her fingers and rubbed more vigorously now in a circular motion, before slipping her middle and index finger inside herself. The water lapped a little inside the tub as she moaned quietly, under the water she could only hear the sound of her own heavy breathing becoming louder and louder. She started to stroke at the hood of her clitoris, she had discovered that she was extremely sensitive there and decided she wanted to take her time. A thought suddenly entered her head that maybe she should have let rob take her virginity after all, if sex could feel this good. But several friends had told her that sex very rarely lives up to the expectations of what a

152

woman can do to herself. She was told by Margaret and Eve that the few times they had done it with guys it wasn't pleasurable, to quote Margaret 'It was wham, bam thank you ma'am!' Eve had added 'He just prodded that thing in and out for five minutes then it was over. I got nothing out of it.'

So in her eyes she didn't want a selfish five minute romp in the backseat of some jock's car, she wanted it to mean something and an experience that would be gratifying to both parties. She slipped the now prune like tip of her middle finger over her clitoris and bit her bottom lip, her thighs quivered causing her knees to kiss.

A cold breeze fluttered across the top of the water and made her stop. It felt as though a draft had blown in from somewhere, as if the door had been opened. She sat up and cradled her breasts with her arm like a sling, concealing her modesty if anyone had walked in. Looking behind her at the door she saw nothing. Nobody was there and the door remain closed. The bathroom was still filled with mist from the heat of the bath and it bathed the whole room in an eery shroud.

She slowly sank back down again and tried to get back into the mood, but the moment had passed and she sighed heavily.

Sophie suddenly had the uncomfortable feeling that she was not alone and she bolted up again, bath water flailing everywhere. She looked around the room and that mist made it difficult for her to make things out. Her eyes widened when she saw a figure in the one corner of the room, but as she focussed she realised that it was just the outline of the water heater tank.

She laughed at her own paranoia "Stop being an idiot!" She scoffed as she gazed around the room and then met another large shape cut

153

into the mist "There's nobody in here!"

Her eyes doubled in size as the shape moved and came out of the mist.

The broad stature of a hulking man filled the corner of the room and he began to slink towards her. She sat frozen thinking it must be a dream. In a moment she would wake up in the tub, a memory popping in her head of her mother telling her how dangerous it was to fall asleep in the tub.

The figure kept moving towards her, the mist evaporating around him. His dirty wet boots squelching with every step. She saw the stained and ripped checkered shirt and dirty shredded Gillet clinging to a beast of a man. A dirty beard, brown and greasy and flecked with grey, but most disturbingly of all, that beard was matted with dried blood. But amazingly it wasn't this that terrified her, nor the scars and divots carved into his large bulbous cranium. It was his eyes that scared her the most, his dark eyes that she stared at feeling like she was falling into them, but there was no bottom to this black abyss. She thought that if you fell in, you would continue to fall forever.

He smiled at her, the few tusk like ivories sprouting in all direction, tipped her over the edge and she tried to scream, but he was on her, a large dirty mitt wrapped around her throat, immediately blocking off the alarm call. His frost bitten blackish fingers squeezed and her face turned an alarming shade of puce, as she gasped for air. He hoisted her from the water like the fresh catch of a fisherman and her naked body hung from his grip. She tried to lash out pawing at his strong arm that never seemed to feel the effects of her blows, the water dripping from her naked body back into the bath as if each droplet was retreating from this hideous creature. Her toes kicked at

154

the surface of the water as they searched aimlessly for something to stand on. It appeared that she was going to pass out or worse be strangled to death, when suddenly he let her go and she fell into the bath. She gasped for air, her long slender neck now bruised and swollen as she hoarsely tried in vain to call for help.

Like a cat with a ball of string he toyed with her, he smiled again a grin that would make one gag, as he caressed her sodden head with his broken shards of nails, that protruded out of his chunky fingertips.

"Please!" Sophie murmured tears filling her eyes now, but it was no good and he grabbed her by the hair and picked her back up again, effortlessly, before plunging her back down into the bathtub headfirst. Her head met the bottom of the cast-iron bath tub and her nose exploded on impact. Blood immediately mixed with the bath water, discolouring it, pinkish and then crimson. Her eyes rolled back in her head as she was trapped under the water, she was revived and then started to struggle realising that she was now being drowned by this demon. He held her under the water for what seemed like and age as her naked body thrashed around like a salmon stranded on the shore. Her hand reached out and grabbed the chain that was attached to the plug and she yanked at it, forcing the plug to leave its dwelling place and let the water escape.

Sophie fought with everything that she had and managed to turn her head in his vice like grip, for air out of the water and with the water rapidly leaving the tub the beast could no longer rely on drowning her. He hoisted her up above his head by her neck and thigh, pressing her small frame effortlessly. She snivelled as she lay helpless above his head in an unbreakable grip. She cried and mumbled words that were incoherent.

He brought her down with rage and velocity, growling as he did so, her back snapping sickeningly over the side of the cast-iron bath. As the cracking of her spinal cord echoed through the bathroom, Sophie died. Her lifeless naked body draped over the side of the bath like a discarded towel, that is where she remained as snowballs continued to explode on the side of the cabin.

CHAPTER 23

The half empty bottle of whiskey hung loosely by its neck in Chopper's grip, swaying two and fro between his legs as he leant forward intently staring into the flames of the past.

"The lumberjacks used to always pack up when the snow came heavy. They were all usually out by the time the first three feet had fallen. It was a sign, you know? Time to leave."

"Yeah!" The Sheriff nodded and finished off his whiskey. Chopper looked at his empty glass cupped in his hands and offered him the bottle.

"Want a top up?"

"I'd better not." The Sheriff smiled.

Chopper turned back to the memory flickering like a video cassette halted on pause, and when he had another swig it started to play out again before him again.

"The freezing of Old Syrup! That was another sign it was time to down tools and head for warmer climes. You know about the freezing of the lake don't you?"

"Yeah! Well, this is my first experience of it, but yeah."

"They say it's so thick it'll hold a man's weight! But, we lost a few kids to Old Syrup back in '88."

"Really?"

"Yeah, A small group of them were horsing around on it,

157

daring each other. You know how it is. Anyway the ice broke and two of them couldn't get out."

"Kid's will be kids I guess." Said Sheriff Russell shaking his head.

"Yeah, we've all done stupid stuff in our youth. But anyway I digress. For what ever reason in the winter of '99, Beau Tooth hadn't made his quota and was behind with his work."

"Any reason for that?"

"It's been speculated that there was trouble at home. His wife Marcy had let slip a few times to Dawn, that he'd gotten a bit overzealous with his belt strap when he'd had a few too many. Others say that it was because his youngest, Abigail, was ill and his head wasn't in the game."

"What was wrong with her?"

"Leukaemia. She was only 5!"

"Jesus! The poor little mite!"

"I guess that's why he drank! Which must have lead to him beating on Marcy and falling behind with his work. But, I'm only clutching at straws here. It's hearsay and bullshit at the end of the day though isn't it? I mean nobody really knows what happened do they? Who knows what the hell goes on behind closed doors!"

"Very true."

"But one thing we do know for sure and that's the outcome."

"And what was that exactly?" Sheriff Russell asked leaning forward, very intrigued by it all now, the way you would when you're watching a good serial on television and you're drawn into the story, too far gone to turn back, you're in it till the end. That's exactly where he was, in it until the end, his heart yearning for it to have a happy ending, but a part of him hoping for a bitter one with all the juicy bits leading to a cliffhanger climax.

There was a pause and Chopper took another swig of whiskey, a long one, he looked like he needed it to unleash this part of the story. Sheriff Russell stared at the whiskey bottle, it seemed to be tilted up for the longest time and he found himself gawking at the muscular physique of the man on the Hackenschmidt label, thinking of his dome like middle aged pot belly and telling himself real people don't look like that. Finally the bottle returned to its swaying cradle in Chopper's hands and what he said next caused all the hairs on Sheriff Russell's neck to stand to attention. Scared stiff almost, every single one of them, he thought they might never return.

"He killed them!" With tears in his eyes he shook his head and turned to The Sheriff, obviously not wanting to catch that part of the imagery in the flames that his imagination had conjured up, it was too much for him. "The bastard hacked them up with his axe!" Sheriff Russell was speechless.

"He beheaded those poor, sweet, innocent little girls." He grizzled openly before returning to the bottle again.

"Oh that's just terrible!" Murmured Sheriff Russell reluctantly painting the horrendous scene in his head.

"That's not even all of it!" Chopper moaned "He cut Marcy's head off too, he did! The fucking bastard! Then you know what the sick fuck did?" Chopper's teary eyes were wide and intense. The pools that hung in his eyelids reflected the raging flames. "He fucking mounted them all on the walls of his cabin!"

"Jesus..." was all Sheriff Russell managed before he felt like vomiting.

159

"Why would he do something like that? What could drive a man to do that to his own family?"

"Who knows for sure!" Chopper shrugged "There are many demons that can seize a man's soul and squeeze it until it is pulp. Some say he just went stir crazy. Being stuck out there all winter can drive a man insane. And a man without sanity has nothing to lose."
There was a pause while all this was being digested by Sheriff Russell. It was a struggle to swallow and he didn't care for the aftertaste.

"Thing is…" Chopper continued "They never found any trace of Beau. It's like he disappeared into thin air."

"Muchnick said he was still out there. What do you think?"

"I don't know. I'd like to think he's rotting in hell for what he's done!"

"Could someone survive out there? In this weather?"

"There's a few theories about this, theories that have been tossed around by the old timers here on a late night drinking session."

"Like what?"

"Some think that he's hiding out in a homemade shack or dugout or possibly a cave. But there's been numerous searches done of Maple Woods and even up to Black Leaf and Blackfoot Ridge and nothing has ever been found. Not a trace!"
Another swig and the bottle is empty. He allows it to fall to the floor, just a short distance from his hanging grip.

"Some also believe that he has a secret hiding place underneath the cabins. But again there's no evidence of this, plus there are numerous visitors to the cabins during the warmer weather and that's what make me suspect that it's the final theory. The one that makes the most sense to me."

"And what would that be?"

"That he's not in Maple Falls at all. Well, at least not all year round."

"What do you mean?"

"Don't you find it curious that all the people who go missing around here, what is it now, 50-60 people since these events?"

"58. 59 if you count the disappearance of Elroy Pascoe."

"Elroy's missing?" Chopper looked at him, his wispy grey eyebrows rising in surprise.

"Yeah! Just a few days!"

"He's dead. He's got to him too!" Chopper sighed shaking his head.

Sheriff Russell didn't know how to respond to that bombshell. In reality he didn't know how to respond to any of it.

"All the disappearances are in the winter time. When the Maple River, Tear Drop and Kowalski all meet up and freeze Old Syrup. That's when people go missing."

"Is that right?" Sheriff Russell says nodding his head slowly, but the police officer inside him thinking that those type of things will have to be checked.

"I know you'll have to check your files and missing persons records, but I guarantee you I'm right."

"I will chase it up as soon as I get to the office."

"Never a trace either is there?"

"Sorry?"

"When you check those files you'll see. Nothing! There's

never a trace of any of them"

"Well, I..."

"And That's another theory!" Chopper interrupts.

"And what's that?"

"That he eats the remains!"

"Fuck..." Sheriff chortled and was about to end the sentence with 'Off!' When he realised that Chopper was serious.

"The remains of his family went missing from the mortuary ambulance shortly after they'd been found."

"Really?"

"Yep! The ambulance was discovered overturned on Maple Way as it was on its way to Maple Grove Hospital. The driver and orderly were killed on impact after ploughing into a redwood."

"So the crash was an accident?"

"No, something blew the tyres."

"Oh!"

"The Tooth family's bodies were missing from the ambulance."

"Shit me!"

"Yep, and as I said, there's been no trace of any of the 58... 59 missing people either."

"Why would he do that?"

"Do what? You're asking me why he kills people and..."

"No!" Sheriff Russell swallows back the nausea before bring himself to say a sentence that he thought he never would have to.

"Why does he... would he eat them?"

"Survival I say. He's a fucking hunter remember. If he's out there somewhere he'll kill and eat them to stay alive."

Sheriff Russell shook his head in disbelief, sinking back into the armchair to try and let it all sink in.

"I'd say he returns every winter to hunt! I mean I don't know anything about cannibalism or how many people a person would be able to live on, but a guy his size he'd have to kill a few a year to keep him in food surely?"

"I have absolutely no clue!"

The two sit in silence shaking their heads for a few moments.

Suddenly Sheriff Russell sits up like a bolt of lightning had hit his ass.

"I've got some kids out there in the woods right now! Staying in one of those cabins! Oh shit!"

"Calm down! They maybe okay. If the theory is correct and Elroy has been claimed by him then they may be safe. He may have filled his quota as it were."

Sheriff Russell stood up and slammed the empty glass on the card table "Theories! I can't base peoples safety on theories!Especially when lives are at stake here!"

"I understand Sheriff, I really do. But don't be too quick to go bounding off into those woods after him. You wouldn't be the first to do that and fail."

With Chopper's words still lingering in the air ,their eyes met and he knew exactly what he meant.

"Sheriff Windwood!" Sheriff Russell said softly "You're talking about him aren't you? He went after him didn't he?"

Chopper dropped his head and nodded.

"Son of a bitch!" Sheriff Russell whispered "I've got to put a stop to this! The people of Maple Falls are in danger!"

"The people of the town are fine."

"What? How can you even say that?"

"Trust me, we're safe."

Sheriff Russell stared at him waiting for him to clarify what he meant, all the time his head bubbling like a pressure cooker of emotions. He knew he had to act and act now!

Chopper remained silent, with seemingly nothing left to add, Sheriff Russell left leaving him to stare aimlessly into the flames.

"The dark deeds we must do to save ourselves." He murmured as a tear rolled down his wrinkled cheek.

CHAPTER 24

The sun had almost set and snow had gently started to fall again on Maple Falls. The swaying redwoods seemed to groan, annoyed at yet another flurry of snow set to smother them.

Cabin number three was silent, as quiet as a graveyard at midnight. Only the sequential dripping of the tap in the kitchen could be heard like the ticking of a clock.

A ruckus of hysterical laughter burst into the cabin as Mia, Max and Dustin fell through the door, collapsing into an uncontrollable sniggering pile in the doorway. All of them covered in snow from dozens of detonated snowballs, their thick goose lined parkers still displaying the residue of them like bruises.

Dustin sat up as the others just lay on the floor a giggling mess "Well, I think he looks kind of sexy!" He smirked looking back out into the snow.

"Oh yeah! Definitely your type, Dust!" Max added sitting up and joining his gaze.

Mia then jumped up and grabbed them both in headlocks playfully "It must be the carrot!" She laughed before they all fell back down in hysterics.

Outside as the snow fell, a double bellied snowman stood proud. Max's scarf tied loosely around his misshapen head, fluttered in the wind and two crooked and dissimilar twigs protruded from its upper body. With coal unavailable, stones that they found made up his smiling mouth and two different coloured rocks becoming his eyes. Dustin's green wooly hat, with a knitted bobble on top had already been blown off and sat in the footprints around the snowman, already being covered with the fresh fallen. A large carrot (the reason for their hysterics) stood at attention from its groin area, playing the part of a large erection.

The door moved in the wind and then Quack and Jessica were there. Smiles etched on their chaffed faces.

"We saw the carrot." Quack smirked "Nice!"

They all laughed as the door was closed behind them and with it that whistling cold wind.

"Max?" Quack addressed him, knowing that penis jokes were his forte "Are you responsible for such childish behaviour?"

"Actually it was Mia!" He laughed and Mia waved at them, one eye almost totally closed now.

"Mia!" Jessica laughed.

Mia shook with suppressed laughter before screeching loudly and keeling over in yet another hysterical fit.

Quack and Jessica looked at each bemused as the three lay at their feet, contorted together like they were in the middle of a hilarious orgy.

"Are you guys stoned?" Jessica asked, but kind of already knowing the answer.

"Never touch it!" Dustin smiled shaking his head.

"They are! Jesus Christ they are!" Quack said shaking his head.

"You guys! If Ms Rougeau finds out, we're dead!" Jessica announced but looking at their ballooned faces as they tried not to laugh just made her giggle.

Quack took her coat and lay it on the sofa, which had become their accustomed coat rack. Quack then kicked off his boots and walked over to Jessica who was struggling to unzip hers with such cold hands.

"Sit!" Quack said to her beaming.

She blushed a little and smiled back before sitting down on one of the chairs around the large table. He knelt down and lifted up her one foot and removed the boot, their eyes never leaving each others. He then did the same to the other and then tossed them over by the sofa nonchalantly.

The floor trifecta had stopped laughing now and became enthralled at what played out before them. Frowns and confused looks did the rounds between them.

Quack stood and held out his hand for Jessica to take it, she did and he hoisted her up "Alley-oop!"

The momentum of him pulling her up off her seat herded her into his waiting arms, obviously by design and the two looked at each other and smiled. Then they kissed passionately and the carpet of collegians gaped in astonishment.

"Damn!" Dustin murmured.

"I really am stoned!" Max gasped "Quack is making out with Jess! Is everybody else seeing this?" He didn't bother to look around as his eyes would not allow themselves to be dragged away from such a spectacle.

"You go girl!" Mia shouted (a sentence she had never once

uttered in her life) before collapsing with yet another outburst of the titters. Quack and Jessica stopped and smiled at each other.

"Right! Whose for something to eat?" Quack announced and was immediately met by three rising hands from the mound on the floor.

"Munchies?" Quack asked, they all nodded in response.

"What's for dinner, chef?" Jessica asked.

"I thought some burgers would go down a treat!" Quack answered "I got a recipe offline called, *Bobby's Burgers*. They look real tasty!"

"Cool. I'll go and see if Sophie wants anything." She stroked his broad back affectionately before skipping away up the stairs.
Quack looked at the rabble on the floor and clapped his hands together "So who's gonna help me prepare dinner?"
They all sank down to the floor in a groan.

The snow fell rapidly and constant as a large frozen carrot was snapped between the grip of frostbitten fingers. The wind hissed with icy saliva over the cabin and the chunky head of a blood besmirched axe ploughed through the head of one poor unfortunate snowman.

CHAPTER 25

Sheriff Russell stood outside the front of the Maple Falls Sheriff Office, his cell phone glued to his ear.

"I know, I know! Look I don't really know what's happening." He said stroking his moustache with his free hand, the way that he did when he was trying to think. "I don't know when I'll be home, no."

He looked through the curtain of constant snow at the high street, everything was closed up for the night now. Everyone had shut up shop and called it a day, all apart from *Chopper's* of course, Sheriff Russell figured that's where most of the shopkeepers were headed after a long working day. The patriotic neon lights flickered on and off advertising Bobby's brand of beer was on tap.

Strangely through thick falling of snow he saw a light on at Dawn's and thought this was very peculiar, she had normally finished up hours before.

"What? Yes, I'm here... and yes I am listening, Holly. But look, seriously now I want you to make sure you lock all the doors up tight!"

A shadowed sauntered across Dawn's Diner and he squinted trying to focus better through the bombardment of falling snow, but he was too far away.

"I'm not being silly. Just do this for me okay?"

He nodded a few times, "I Love you!" and hung up, slotting his cell phone into the pocket of his jacket and zipping it up, all the while not taking his eyes off the diner.

He finally made his way inside the office and was met by Lieutenant Adams who looked concerned. "Is everything okay, Sheriff? You look a little out of it?"

"Long day, Tammy. Long ass day." He sighed, removing his snow clad hat and scratching at his head.

"Tragic about Chuck, Eh?" She said shaking her head.

"Yeah! Did you..." He started to ask a question and Tammy who was always one step ahead knew what he was going to ask.

"Raymond?" She nodded "Yeah, I sent him home. It hit him really hard."

"Yeah, I thought it might."

There was a moment of silence before Tammy chimed back in "Oh! You've had a few messages while you were out."

"Hit me!" He said with more enthusiasm than he would have liked, he really wanted to go home and curl up in a warm bed next to an even warmer wife. Seeing Charles Muchnick's brain matter splattered on the wall was enough for anybody to withdraw from the day, not to mention Chopper's ghost stories, that if were true could spell serious trouble for everyone in Maple Falls. He'd definitely had enough for one day.

"Well, Marlena called again..."

"Marlena?" He murmured, obviously difficult for him to focus when so much was muttering around inside his head.

"Pascoe? She asking if there were any developments with Elroy's disappearance."

"Pretty sure he's dead." He said nonchalantly.

Lieutenant Adams looked at him with wide eyes, that were heavily caked in lilac eyeshadow that had seeped into the crows feet around her wrinkled eyes. "You know that for sure?"

"Nope! Just a wild stab in the dark." He sighed.

"Okay!" She said and frowned again in worry for him. "What else was there? Oh! Nathan has had to leave his shift and go help with a huge fire up in Blackfoot."

"Is that so?"

"Yeah, some mental institute up on Blackfoot Ridge?"

"Yeah, I've heard of it."

"Well, it's gone up in flames! They think it's killed everyone inside. They're having trouble controlling the blaze, so all available fire engines from neighbouring towns have been called in to help."

"Of course. I understand."

"Mack Ferris has had to lead the way with his plough too. So we've no plough tonight if it was needed I'm afraid."

"I don't think we will, to be honest. Is Emily still out?"

"She's still out and now on foot. She called in about an hour or so ago and said her truck was stuck."

"Were her tyres not chained?"

"Afraid not."

"Raymond!" He griped and then sighed realising that he was probably going through his own personal hell and chaining the tyres of the vehicles had slipped his mind completely.

"I'm going to check a few things and then I'm going home. Will you and Emily be okay tonight?"

"I'm sure we will." She smiled and it was a motherly,

171

reassuring smile which actually made him feel a bit better.

"Oh! One more thing before you go!" She said, rummaging through her notes "A Jessica Head called for you?"

"A who?" He asked, shaking his head like the name has never had any meaning to him.

"Jesica Head was the name she had given."

"Never heard of her."

"She's one of the kids stopping up at the cabin?"

"Oh!" His eyes saucer like and his heart skipped a beat "Is everything okay up there?"

"Well, yeah! I mean I think so. She was very sweet and polite, but she did sound a little worried. You see one of the girls found a stag's head in bed with her this morning!"

"Excuse me?"

"The head of a stag? A deer! The head of a dead deer!"

"Fuck!" He said and then his mind drifted off, thinking the worst.

"Yeah, I thought it was pretty weird too. She said they don't know who put it there."

"I think I'm going to have to go up there!"

"I can come with you if you wish, Sheriff?"

"No! You're needed here, Tammy."

He placed his hat back on his head, moist melting flakes fell off it as he fitted back into place.

"She said that she called Dawn, but the line was bad and then she couldn't get through. That's why she called here."

"Are the lines down?"

"No! I mean they won't get a cell signal out there. But, the

172

cabin phone was working fine at their end."

"Right..." He spoke quietly and already miles away, his eyes squinted out through the misting window and over at the light that still remained on at Dawn's Diner.

"You okay?"

"Yeah... I'm going to check on Dawn and then I'm going to make sure those kids are okay."

He opened the door to leave and the cold relentless wind and snow attacked him, snipping at his face, causing him to squint and turn away from the barrage. Before he stepped out into the cold abyss, he turned to Tammy who sat behind the reception desk still watching him intently, probably sighing with relief inside that he didn't take her up on her offer of coming with him.

"Have you ever heard of Beau Tooth?"

He asked staring wildly at her, looking for any lying twitch of her face that may give her away.

"No!" She shrugged "Can't say I have."

"Right." He said quietly, his mind drifty away.

"Should I have?" She asked with all sincerity.

He believed her, then realised that Tammy Adams had only lived in Maple Falls herself for around eight years or so, so she wouldn't be in on it, if there was actually anything to be in on.

"It doesn't matter!" He said as he disappeared into the whiteness.

CHAPTER 26

Max unleashed and almighty belch that shook the mounted trophies peering down at him. He lent back in his chair and clutched his full stomach with both hands.

"Oh Quack!" He groaned "Will you marry me?"

The table laughed, all mirroring Max in patting their stuffed guts in satisfaction. All but Jessica, who had taken some food up to Sophie's room.

"Was it that good?" Quack asked.

"Oh yeah! Baby!" Max said closing his eyes and leaning even further back in his chair.

"You'll definitely have to add that to your repertoire." Mia said, dabbing at her lips with a napkin.

"You'll need a better name though." Dustin intervened "I mean you can't call it Bobby's Burgers… You're not a Bobby!"

"Any suggestions?" Quack asked shaking his head that wore a proud cheesy grin, his double chin wobbling as he shook.

"Duckworth's 'Girthy' Burger!" Dustin spat in jest.

"Jesus!" Quack laughed "I can just see that on a menu!"

"It can't be anything with 'Girthy' in the title for God's sake!" Mia added "How about Big boy's…"

"Pretty sure that's been done!" Dustin intervened "What are you gonna say next? 'Big Mac?" He scoffed.

174

They shared playful grimaces and stuck their tongues out at each other.

"I've got it!" Max said with authority and stood up from his chair thumping a fist down on the table.

"Then let's hear it, Maximus!" Quack said preparing himself by sitting back and folding his arms. The chair squealed for mercy under his hefty bulk, but managed to keep itself together.

Max cleared his throat and looked up to the ceiling, building the anticipation. He took a deep breath and said "The Big Quack!" spreading his hands out above his head to emphasise the name in lights.

"Bravo!" Quack said standing up applauding, Dustin and Mia followed suit and applauded and cheered. Max took a bow.

"You guys!" Jessica said walking down the stairs and stopping half way "Sophie's asleep!"

They all immediately stopped their rowdy antics and sat back down.

"We're sorry, Jess." Quack said.

"As she actually ventured from her crypt today?" Mia scoffed.

"Yeah, I think she owes us all apologies!" Dustin added.

"I tapped the door, but there was no answer. So I left her a plate of food outside her room."

"Yummy! Seconds!" Max said licking his lips and rubbing his hands together like some dastardly villain who had just tied the damsel to the railroad tracks and was expecting a speeding locomotive at any moment.

"No Max!" Jess said shaking her head "You'll leave it for Soph!"

"Okay." Max sulked.

"Are you sure she's in there? I haven't seen her all day! Perhaps she's gone too? Took after Rob perhaps." Dustin said.

"Don't know." Jessica shrugged "I didn't really want to disturb her. I'm sure she is feeling pretty shitty about everything at the moment and just needs some time alone."

They all nodded in agreement.

"She's had a bath though" Jess added "Bathroom is in a right state! I don't know what she has been up to in there."

"Oh, well!" Quack said standing up and starting to pile up the empty plates "What's on the agenda this evening? Another marathon of *Dungeons and Dragons*? Or I did see a *Scrabble* in the cupboard?"

"There's too many of us for scrabble." Max chimed in.

"Well, you and Dustin can team because the pair of you combined would make one brain, right?" Mia smiled.

"Okay, Cyclops, cool it!" Max laughed.

"I was planning to show Mia my pro wrestling card collection!" Dustin beamed with excitement.

"Oh great! I thought I'd dodged that bullet?" She said rolling her one good eye.

"Well, before you do any of that you can all sort out the dishes." Jessica announced to a chorus of boos.

"Quack, could I see you upstairs about something, please?" Jessica asked, her face glowing in slight nervous embarrassment. The mouths in the room gawped, Quack's too, even lower if it was possible.

"Yeah! Yeah sure!" He said walking towards her "Is

everything okay?" He asked as he reached the stairs.

"Everything's great!" She answered and wandered off ahead of him. He stood there for a moment, his meaty hand gripping the newel post. He took a step up and the stair creaked loudly. He turned to see everyone looking at him and smiling.

"Go get her, big guy!" Mia smiled.

Max and Dustin had other methods of showing their support as Max bent Dustin over the table and simulated anal sex by thrusting his groin into his buttock area.

"Feed me Big Quack, feed me!" Dustin groaned comically.

"Jesus!" Quack laughed and then swallowed, he thought his Adam's apple was going to touch his testicles before it suddenly popped back into place and with a nervous exhale he strode up the stairs.

"Well, how about that?" Dustin said shaking his head.

"Well, their night's planned. What are we gonna do then?" Max added.

"Guys?" Mia said and their attention was drawn to her.

They both smiled as she held in her hand another doobie.

CHAPTER 27

Sheriff Russell wiped the sleeved of his jacket across the window of the diner, removing the layer of crystallisation that had built up from the snow. He peered inside and saw Dawn lying in a foetal position on the checkerboard tiles, like the king piece in a game of chess, dejected, down, beaten, checkmate.

"Shit!" He growled and moved towards the door he pushed against it heavily, expecting it to be locked, but was very surprised when it flung open and he careened inside.

"Dawn?" He yelled and ran to her side.

She shuddered and tears ran down her face, her body convulsing with each laboured breath.

"Dawn!" Sheriff Russell sighed. A sigh of relief, his initial thought being that she was dead. "What's wrong? What's happened to you?" He asked with concern as he knelt down and lifted her head up from the ground, tiny pieces of broken glass stowed away in the greying mass, hair that had started the day in a neat bun, but was now in disarray and cascading down and clinging to her moist flush cheeks.

"Oh, Patrick... please forgive me!" She sobbed.

"What is it?" He asked, rocking her back and forth, trying to comfort her.

She did not answer, she just went on crying and sniffing. She snivelled and was seemingly unconsolable.

Sheriff Russell wiped the tear drenched strands of hair away from her face. Cheeks streaked with mascara and red lipstick smudged. He looked at her for any signs that she had been attacked. A bruise, a cut, a graze, anything! Anything to give him some sort of idea on what had happened to her.

There was nothing. No marks on her that would indicate that anything physical had taken place. He looked around and saw the telephone had been ripped away from the wall and lay lifeless and useless on the floor by the counter. His brow furrowed and his eyes searched the diner for more evidence.

"What has gone on here, Dawn? You must tell me!"

The fragmented picture frame surrounded by shards of broken glass. He turned the frame over and saw that photograph again.

The Bear Busters.

His eyes focussed on Beau Tooth and was lost in a moment of wonderment.

What if it was all true? Everything that Muchnick said... Everything that Chopper had told him. Could it really be true? Is there a maniacal lumberjack out there hunting the people of Maple Falls?

He placed the frame back on a bed of glass and looked at Dawn again, who's snivelling had now been subdued and were replaced by moist sniffs of her flaring nostrils. She finally looked up at him with raw eyes and sniffed again. Her red nostrils flared again, opening and closing like the mouth of a trout that had found itself in the hands of a fisherman and gasping for air.

"I'm so sorry for what I've done, Patrick. I really am!"

"What is it you've done, Dawn? None of this makes any sense to me?"

"Beau Tooth has returned!" She shook with fear as she mentioned his name. It was passed through trembling lips and her body followed suit. He felt her fear as he held her, still rocking her like a sick infant.

"He can't be out there, Dawn. Not after all this time. He would have died out there in the wilderness!" He said, trying to convince himself more than Dawn.

"Well, I don't know where he goes too, Patrick. But I tell you he's back!" And with that she grabbed his forearm with both her hands, gripping so tightly he could feel her fingernails digging into his flesh. He winced and held one of her hands to stop her, she squeezed it tightly.

"Elroy Pascoe is dead!" Dawn whispered "He's taken him."

"We don't know that for sure, Dawn!"

"And those kids. Those poor kids! They found a... sign!"

"The Stags head. I know. They telephoned the station when they couldn't get through to you." His eyes glanced again at the broken telephone.

"Oh God!" She cried again. This time the tears seemed different, something different in her cry. Not fear, not pain but guilt. Cries of guilt.

"Look if he's really here and killing people, I have to put out an announcement to the town."

"No!" She screamed. Her voice echoed around the empty diner and startled him. She sat up and glared at him.

"The people of Maple Falls are safe...I've..." She paused for a moment and lowered her head in shame "...I've taken care of that."

He looked at her for the longest time his forehead corrugated with the ripples of confusion. Then she looked at him again, her eyes welling, like two snow globes about to be shaken up.

"I've taken care of it and I'm so very, very sorry." She sobbed.

Then he heard the quiet lingering voice of Bruce Hardwood, something he said as he left the backroom at the bar, at first he thought he hadn't heard him correctly, but now it made sense.

"The dark deeds we must do to save ourselves." He said the words out loud and then the realisation hit him and hit him hard. It was though Mack Ferris' snowplough had just driven through him. He actually toppled backwards and fell on his behind, joining Dawn on the cold checkerboard tiles. Checkmate.

"Oh my God, Dawn!" He said cupping a gloved hand over his mouth "Those kids...Those poor kids!"

He grabbed her by the shoulders and shook her "Those fucking kids!" He screamed at her, spitting all over her as she sobbed again.

"I know, I know, I'm so sorry. It was the only way!" She cried shaking her head in shame "Can't you see? It's the only way!"

"You set them up! You sacrificed those innocent kids didn't you?"

She cried again.

"Didn't you!" He yelled.

She cried more unwilling to allow herself to say the word.

"Damn you Dawn!" He shook her again "You did, didn't you!"

"YES!" She finally relented and yelled back "It was the only way to keep the town safe." She blubbered and he let her go of her, disgusted at her. Her body slid back to the ground almost lifelessly and he stood up and wiped his hand over his face.

"What the hell have you done!" He murmured.

Again those words manifested in his head.

"The dark deeds we must do to save ourselves."

CHAPTER 28

Quack sat up in his bed, shirtless, but with the covers pulled up to meet his roll of chins, nervously covering his modesty. He knew he was obese and he wasn't entirely sure that Jess would want to see him naked. Second thoughts struck home like a hammer to the head. But then the soothing vocals of *Norah Jones* crept from the speaker that had Jessica's cell phone attached to it. She turned to him and smiled and as those splendid lyrics of *Sunrise* caressed his ears he lowered his guard and smiled back. She walked over to the bed and when she sat beside him and touched his hand, he quivered. She kissed him. It felt to him like electricity had just shot up his spine, he became covered in a layer of gooseflesh. His heart felt warm, like it had never felt before as their lips met and she stroked his chubby face with the soft caress of her hand. If he was completely honest he felt like crying. He had never felt this cherished in his whole life.

She stopped kissing him and pulled away smiling. She held the top of sheet and attempted to remove it but his anxiety kicked in again and he tightened his grip it.

"Quack?"

"I don't think you want to see that." He said in a moment of bashful self loathing.

"I want to see you!" She said and kissed him again a little

before pulling away and stroking his face once again "I want to see all of you!"

"Are you sure?" He asked meekly, wearing that mask of embarrassment again, the one he donned on a daily basis. In the locker room at college. On the beach at summer time. Even a barrage of insults in his own house from family members when he is eyed leaving the bathroom in just a towel.

"Trust me, Quack. Please!" She said softly grasping the sheets and smiling again "I would never hurt you."

He believed her and let go. He let go of everything.

He closed his eyes as he lay naked, a lumpy misshapen mass, with tufts of dark hair sprouting from his chest and around his small flaccid penis. He felt like crying again, this time out of humiliation. He thought that it was all going to turn out to be some joke and everyone was going to barge in laughing and pointing at him, all his personal inadequacies on display for all to see.

He squeezed his eyelids together tightly awaiting the inevitable moment that she would laugh at him, but the laughter never came. She kissed him again and caressed his flesh with her soft warm hands. He relaxed and there was a moment of stirring in his loins. She whispered in his ears "Now, let me show you!"

He opened his eyes as she stepped back away from the bed, her face glowing in coyness. She unbuttoned her jeans and let them fall to the floor, she stepped out of them and then worked her underwear down slowly. The length of her shirt covered her private parts as she stood back up and playfully threw her underwear at him.

He smiled and she giggled.

That electricity was flowing through his body again, this time to the

184

tip of his penis.

He wanted it to happen, Oh boy did he ever, but again there was that feeling of worthlessness and inadequacy that stopped it from happening. That doubt, that strong rock of doubt that we all pull around with us everyday. Sometimes we just have to cut that rope and leave that rock to lay.

Fuck it! He thought to himself and took his mind off trying to rise anything, whether it be stones, spaceships sunken in swamps or indeed dicks.

She started to unbutton her shirt and he saw her, he saw her flesh, it was perfect. Untouched and perfect like an ivory statue. She breathed in and then let her inhibitions leave with the falling shirt. She quickly slipped off her bra while she was feeling brave and stood there for him to see. She blushed and tried to stand as natural as one could while they're naked in front of someone. Her breasts were pert and the cold draft that worked its way under the door made her nipples firm. Jessica thought that they were too small.

Her stomach quivered under the attack of a thousand goosebumps.

She hated her stomach, she thought it was bloated and stuck out too much.

She looked down and her eyes widened, she had forgotten to give her pubic hair a trim and to her it was as wild as a gooseberry bush. In reality the area looked perfectly natural.

"You're b-beautiful." He stuttered and all those doubts went away.

She smiled and walked towards him. His dick was now hard, it had snook up on him while he wasn't thinking about it and before he could worry about something else she climbed on top of him, and kissed him.

They kissed passionately for what felt like twenty minutes it was in fact maybe two at the most. They were cautiously dancing around the inevitable, her vagina skimming the top of his penis as they both were consumed with doubt again.

They stopped kissing and looked into each others frightened eyes. This time no words were needed to soothe the others doubts. They both knew that everything was going to be fine.

She gently sat down and after a startled but pleasant sound escaped her lips she smiled at him. Quack realised that he was holding his breath and exhaled loudly, which made Jess laugh, he smiled too knowing that the laughter wasn't at him because of how he looked, but because they were both in the same boat. They both had the same doubts in life, and at this moment in time they both felt the same way about each other.

She started to writhe her hips as she sat on top of him. He began to thrust slowly, it was all very natural to them, but new to them at the same time as their wet genitals harmonised.

"Okay?" She asked.

"Yeah! You?"

She nodded.

"Nice?" He whispered.

"Yeah! For you?"

She blushed and nodded again.

She started to move faster and he followed suit with the speed of his thrusts to match hers. She groaned and closed her eyes.

"Are you okay?" He asked in concern.

"Uh-huh!" She groaned.

"Does it hurt?"

"Nuh-uh!"

She sat up and arched her back, as she squirmed vigorously back and forth on top of him. Her pert breasts stood out longing to be touched, they bounced up and down slightly with each thrust of his penis (A penis he thought was always too small but it was doing the job today). He grabbed her breasts and her face contorted with discomfort. He apologised for his heavy handedness, his sausage like fingers had never before touched the tender flesh of a breast before. She smiled and he caressed them gently, watching them, almost fascinated by the shapes that they made in his hands. He was that hypnotised by her breasts that his ejaculation snuck up on him and took him by surprise. Jessica seemed to sense it coming and moved faster still, on the verge of coming herself, probably not yet realising that she was in the minority of the 18% of women that can come from penetrative sex. She managed to climax just as he was finishing, it may have been those few final long thrusts from Quack that sealed the deal. She dismounted and lay next to him, both of their bodies a little tacky with sweat. They sat in silence as *Norah Jones* made way to *Lionel Richie's, Do It to Me.*

They both burst into a fit of laughter and turned to each other kissing and cuddling.

"Well, How about it?" Jessica asked.

"How about what?"

"Doing it to me one more time?" She laughed.

He cuddled her and knew that at that moment he loved her.

"You may have to give me a few minutes." He laughed.

"Well, studies have shown around fifteen." She giggled.

"Okay, smart ass!" He kissed her again "I best go to the John and we can try again? That's if you want to?"

"Of course you big galoot! That was lovely and I want do it again."

He climbed out of bed, peeping out from under his rotund belly was his dick still throbbing up and down as though it was panting, running on empty. He pulled on his sweat pants and grabbed his favourite T-shirt, his lucky tattered *Return of the Jedi* shirt, and then blew her a kiss.

"I love you!" He said and then stopped wide eyed with the realisation of what just left his lips.

She climbed to her knees still naked but totally comfortable and met him at his level planting a little kiss on the end of his round nose.

"It's okay, Quack. Because I think I love you too!"

They smiled at each other.

"I think I always have." She added "And I'm so glad I got to do this with you. That you were my first, and hopefully my only."

They embraced and kissed again and Quack left for the bathroom.

Quack almost skipped down the corridor, If a guy of his size could really skip. He moved into the bathroom and locked the key in the door behind him. He yanked down his sweats and lowered himself down onto the toilet. His dick had started to lower now and recharge its batteries, he looked at it and smiled "You did good my young apprentice." He scoffed, laughing to himself.

The door handle rattled as though somebody was coming in. Quack looked up from his porcelain throne and glanced at the door directly ahead.

"I'm in here, guys!"

The doorknob jerked again.

"I think I'm gonna be a while."

The doorknob jerked again violently and for a longer duration.

"What the fuck, guys! Give it a rest will ya!"

There was silence and then nothing.

"A guy can't even have a shit in peace these days!"

The doorknob rattled and shook again, violently as if it was going to fall off at any moment.

"Shit!" Quack yelled and it stopped.

Silence.

"Jerks!" He said shaking his head and then started thinking about what an amazing experience he had just had. How he thought that all his anxieties and worries had fluttered away while he was with her.

He thought to himself it was a pretty cool deal falling in love.

The key suddenly flung itself out of the keyhole as though someone had skewered it from the other side. It sang as it hit the hard tiled floor and he sat looking at the key in bewilderment. He gazed closely at the keyhole and very slowly he saw something enter the hole. It was a screwdriver, a cross head.

"What the hell?" Quack whispered as he stared at it.

Suddenly it was violently jammed at the lock and the door swung open. The gargantuan frame of Beau Tooth stood in the door way and he smiled that crooked smile, his dark eyes shimmering like hematite in the twitch of the fluorescent strip light.

"Who in the..." Quack started to say but was immediately silenced by the large bloodied axe that hung from a chapped right hand.

For a moment Quack was frozen in fear on the toilet. All the positive pep talk he'd given his penis minutes ago meant nothing, because it had shrunken down and nestled in a mass of dark pubic hair.

Beau Tooth had to bend down and contort his huge frame to even enter the room, then the door was closed slowly behind him. The axe head hit the tiled flooring, a tile split from the impact and a crack was formed diagonally from corner to corner. Slowly he slunk towards him, the sound of the axe's head singing across the tiles was horrendous, it was then that Quack realised this was no joke and he attempted to grab his sweat pants and pulled them up, but with three bounding strides Beau Tooth was on him.

The first strike from the axe drove down between his neck and his shoulder, taking a chunk out of his trapezius muscle before the axe was yanked back out.

Quack couldn't scream as he winced with pain and sat back on the toilet grabbing at his wound. His chubby face looked panic struck as he saw his own blood gush from the wound and being soaked up by his favourite T-Shirt.

The second strike came down on the very top of his head and shattered his skull, this would have caused immediate brain and nerve damage. His body jiggled as he leant all the way back and rested against the toilet's tank. He was now open to anything this hellion lumberjack wanted to dish out.

The third strike wedged into his torso, the fourth cracked through his sternum, the fifth destroyed his ribcage that was hiding under a pile of soft blubber. The ribs continued to snap and crack, sounding like the breaking of stale breadsticks.

There were 32 relentless violent lacerations in total as metal met flesh, then bone and then bowels.

The sound of the blood soaked axe hitting and breaking another tile could be heard as it was discarded.

Beau Tooth's breathing was heavy as he stood and stared at the tenderised corpse of Chester Duckworth. His head tilted from side to side as he calculated just how he was he going to move such a colossal agglomeration.

Meanwhile, Jessica had fallen asleep.

CHAPTER 29

Sheriff Russell cursed his Deputy, Raymond Clegg several times, as he moved at speed towards the Maple Woods. He also besieged himself with expletives, knowing full well that Raymond couldn't be blamed for not having the trucks wheels chained and ready. A good friend of his had just committed suicide and he needed to go home and get his head straight. Sheriff Russell thought that's exactly what he needed to do as well, with everything he'd gone through today. But when you're the Sheriff the buck stops with you. There's no time outs or breaks for Sheriff Russell, he has to keep going.

The Bobcat was fast, he clung to its handle bars as it skipped along on top of the deep snow. The falling snow harassed him like a swarm of wasps, stinging his face with relentless glacial abandon.

The Bobcat brand snowmobile was a firm favourite for all at the Sheriff's Office. Everyone was always eager to take the Bobcat out and Sheriff Russell was usually just as eager as the rest of them, but not tonight. He really wished the circumstances were different and that he could be a million miles away from here, a nice warm beach perhaps? Even sitting at home on the sofa sipping at a hot chocolate would do. Instead he found himself on the snow covered road that lead to those cabins.

To be perfectly honest there may not be anything wrong and it may well be the people of Maple Falls that are deranged. These are things that had gone through his mind but they were merely what if's made up by his own psyche trying to tell him everything was fine. His gut told him differently. His gut churned, mulling over all the information he had taken in that day, and the answer it had given him was trouble.

He came off Maple Way, which had now become treacherous for travellers out and about without chains and as he whizzed past at high speed he noticed a few vehicles abandoned on the side of the road. With Mack Ferris over at Blackfoot Ridge that meant no ploughing would take place tonight. He thought that maybe he should check the stranded vehicles in case anyone was in them. But he didn't. That gut instinct was yanking on his intestines and all he could think about was those kids.

He took a sharp righthand turn and because of the speed he was running at he had to fight with the machine to keep it from toppling over. The bright yellow hood shuddered, the spindles holding the ski's almost bowed as the track kicked up a violent squall and snow was splattered against the large redwoods that frame the drive up to the cabins. The engine buzzed annoyingly as he hurtled towards his destination. He actually smirked to himself, reliving that moment of déjà vu, that he was doing exactly the same journey last night. How ironic he thought to himself and then wished that he had had all this information last night.

Those kid's would have been soon out of there! Whether they wanted to leave or not! I'd have made damn sure of it.

The bobcat's single vanilla headlight lead the way through the darkness. The contrast of the black and white surroundings was almost captivating.

Finally up ahead he could see the lights from the cabin in the distance, flickering through the shroud of falling snow like a lighthouse warning of threatening jagged rocks that awaited oncoming ships.

For a moment his head seemed elsewhere, he thought of his wife Holly, probably already curled up in front of the boob-tube watching some forgotten classic from *Hammer*. He thought about how much he loved her, he found himself reminiscing about the good times they'd spent together and how sad it was that they never had any children. He felt as though he was going away. The vision of Charles Muchnick's brain matter sliding down the wall of his trailer, shook him out of his trance and for a moment he fought against the urge to vomit or cry, or maybe even both. He thankfully did neither.

As he adjusted his numb posterior on the long slender seat he hit something under the snow. The ski immediately snapped and the engine howled like an animal in pain. The Bobcat flipped and sent Sheriff Russell hurtling into the trees. His head struck an unforgiving redwood and he was knocked out, cold.

The engine of the Bobcat began to die, the headlight dimmed with it and leaking gasoline worked its way around its mechanical carcass like a moat. Sheriff Russell lay unconscious in a snow angel pose as the flakes began to smother him, covering up the sins of the woods once again, like it always had and always will.

CHAPTER 30

Sniggering laughter again filled the main room of the cabin as the unsuspecting trio of Mia, Max and Dustin played truth or dare, as they passed around the smouldering remains of yet another doobie.

The fire raged on behind them as Max and Dustin sat on the bear skin rug as Mia sat wrapped up in what had become 'her chair'.

"Flash me your tits!" Max squeaked and Dustin joined him in shrieking laughter.

"You little pervert!" Mia scoffed a look of surprise on her face, as her one good eye widened, the other concealed by two bulging purple eyelids.

"You gotta do it!" Max said taking another long drag, his eyes disappearing into the back of his head.

"Like hell I have!" Mia yelled back.

"It's that or you have to pay the piper! Or It'll be a dare for you!" Max scoffed and passed the filtering doobie to Dustin who took a drag too.

"What's the dare?" Mia sighed.

"You have to streak outside."

"No way!" She shook her head.

"Yep, you complete one circuit around the cabin or you have to flash your boobies!" Max sang almost triumphantly.

195

"Boobies, Boobies, Boobies!" Dustin chanted.

Mia thought it over. She didn't really want to do either, even if the Marijuana had loosened her usual rigid temperament. She thought a quick flash of her breast would be better than a naked canter outside in the freezing cold.

"Okay!" She announced.

The cheers rose and touched the ceiling.

"I'll show you them. But, on one condition!"

"What's that?" Max asked.

"If you do the streak!"

Dustin laughed and collapsed pointing at Max who sat there for a moment pondering the offer.

"I'll do it!" He shouted already pulling off his socks.

"Really?" Came the surprised chorus from his friends in unison.

"Yep!" He announced "It'll be worth it for a peak at Chung's Guns!"

"You're such a creep!" She said and then laughed. She positioned herself on the edge of the armchair and removed the fur skins that was keeping her comfortable. Max and Dustin leant forward, now like two anticipating children waiting for a story from a teacher. Her breasts were quite large and sat behind a thick sweatshirt with the letters 'SCU' emblazoned on it. She clutched the bottom of her sweater and waited, shaking her head as she comprehended what she was about to do.

"I can't believe I'm doing this!" She sighed.

Max and Dustin's eyes widened.

"Wait!" Mia said, causing Max and Dustin to exhale, all their

196

pent up excitement evaporating.

"What?" Max moaned "You can't back out! I've already taken my socks off!"

"How long?" She asked.

"It'll be about 7 inches in a minute!" Dustin scoffed.

"Very funny!" Mia said and then her   face contorted as she thought about Dustin's last statement "Seven? You're dreaming!"
Max laughed at Dustin.

"How long do I have to flash them for?"

"10 Seconds!" Max announced.

"Hell no! That's way too long! I was thinking more along the lines of 3!"

"3? Make it 5 and we have a deal!" Max said taking the butt of the doobie from Dustin and sucking the remaining life from it before tossing it into the fire, its remains burning up into black ash immediately.

"Okay!" She agreed and tightly grasped the bottom of the sweater again. She closed her good eye and yanked it up swiftly. Her breasts were dragged up by the sweater and then fell into a heavy bounce where they sat bathed by the light of the fire.
Max and Dustin's eyes protruded on stalks and their lips mouthed a slow count to five as they took each precious second to paint a mental picture that would stay with them until their end of days.

"Five!" Mia cried and brought the sweater down like the drawbridge of a medieval castle, dampening the duo's harder.
They groaned.

"Now it's your turn, Maximus!" Mia said smugly.

"Fine!" He said, the vision of her large breasts bouncing out from underneath her sweater replaying in his head on a loop. The trousers came off and then the sweater and he was soon down to his underwear, and without even a second thought he whipped them off too. Mia and Dustin sat in awe with the ease that he did it and he stood there with his hands on his hips like some super hero, his flaccid penis already fearing the cold and hibernating as the fire lit his naked and scrawny physique.

"Ta da!" He shouted and he was off into the night, opening the door and gliding into the flurry of snow that attacked his exposed flesh. The door slammed behind him and Mia and Dustin doubled over with laughter.

There was a pause and Mia looked at Dustin who was staring at her.

"You're still thinking about my breasts aren't you?" She asked.

"No!" He said shaking his head "I wanna show you my cards."

"Oh Brother!" She whined leaning back in her chair and cocooning herself up with the skins once again.

"Go on then!" She sighed "I'm not going to get any peace and quiet until you do, am I?"

"Nope!" He smiled.

Outside Max trotted through the knee high snow, shivering ridiculously and thinking to himself whether this was one of his stupidest ideas ever. There was no way of explaining just how cold his body was. His teeth chattered as he turned the first corner of the cabin, his enthusiasm had been immediately halted by the coldness and his trot had slowed to a trudge.

"Damn! It's freezing!" He shuddered.

He stopped in the snow for a second, falling sleet sweeping against his pimpled flesh and then smiled.

"It was totally worth it though!" He laughed as he carried on with his lap of honour.

"Did you see those monsters jiggle!" He laughed to himself "Amazing!"

He suddenly heard a loud noise that slowed his progress. The sound was loud like a gunshot he thought initially, then thought it was more like wood striking on wood. He heard it again as it echoed through the dark woods.

"Anyone there?" He called out into the night and the only response he was met by was his own voice echoing back at him, before it was quickly eaten up by the harsh wind.

He continued around the corner and saw the woodshed door was open and with each flurrying gust of wind it was colliding with a pile firewood stacked next to it.

He decided that he would shut the door or else nobody was going to get any sleep that night.

He shut the door and let out a shriek as he came face to face with a bloodied hatchet that was rammed into the door.

"What the hell!" He murmured. Just then another hatchet came hurtling past his head and sank into the door, the wood splintering around its bloody blade. He span around on the spot to see Beau Tooth standing near the cabin. The figure of Tooth was difficult to make out in the shadow of the cabin, that smothered him. But Max saw the shine of yet another hatchet blade. His eyes grew wide in frozen terror, but before he could scream that third hatchet cut through the air and buried itself into scrawling bare chest. The velocity that the hatchet was thrown at caused Max to become pinned to the door. He struggled to breathe and could only manage a squeak as blood started to emerge from his chest and was cascading down his naked body. He swallowed hard and was about to pluck up all he had to try and scream for help when he was met by a tirade of hatchets in quick succession all meeting their targets. His face, his thigh, his left shoulder, the last one tore through his cold timid penis.

The last remnants of life left his body in a spectre of vapour that quickly dissipated in the heavy flurry of flakes.

His lifeless naked body hung to the door, the aggressive wind still managing to make the door judder slightly, even under the deadweight of Max Fellows' carcass.

The lacerations on his exposed corpse were gently kissed by the crisp snowflakes, causing his oozing plasma and entrails to coagulate.

His eyes glazed over with a layer of frozen sleet and his pale flesh already looked brushed with a subtle pastel shade of blue.

CHAPTER 31

Sheriff Russell started to stir. Covered in a layer of snow he rose from its numbing shroud shuddering profusely, immediately he groaned and seized his throbbing head in his gloved hands.

His Ushanka headwear had long gone, falling off as he unceremoniously left the Bobcat. It could be anywhere now, lost to the unrelenting snowstorm that consumed Maple Woods. But losing his hat was of course the least of his worries as he removed his glove and dabbed at his tender forehead with his fingers, checking for a wound. Luckily there was no blood, but there was a swollen bulge protruding from it, resembling an eggplant in both colour and shape.

"Shit!" He hissed his fingertips touching it tentatively as he tried to take in his whereabouts. He pulled himself out of the Patrick Russell shaped divot in the mound of snow and stretched his cold aching body. His joints creaking wildly, almost mimicking the sound of those gigantic redwoods that swayed from side to side above him. Glancing around something caught his eye, something gleaming through the snow smothered wilderness. Something that didn't quite belong. He pushed himself through the snow towards what ever treasure lay hidden between the brambles. When he reached the start of the trees he'd noticed that there were a number of disturbed branches, some of them broken. To the untrained eye this wouldn't have appeared out of the ordinary, a rambler may have taken it for a bear moving through the thicket, or a moose perhaps. But, Sheriff Russell did own a trained eye, he actually owned two of them and what he saw with them is that something larger had forced its way through and it was that that was blinking at him in the darkness.

It didn't take him long to reach the black Dodge that was concealed by foliage and snow. He wiped away the drivers side window and peered inside, there was nothing.

"Elroy Pascoe!" He whispered, his breath fogging up the area he'd just wiped.

He pulled himself out of the thicket and back onto the drive, he looked up the untouched road of white that lead the way up to the cabins. The lights could still be seen as if flickering an SOS through the constant fall of snow.

"About thirty minutes on foot." He told himself, stopping himself from speaking those words that pirouetted on his moist tongue, twirling and spinning along his chapped bottom lip and then disappearing back inside, never to be spoken. But he thought it.

I hope I'm not too late.

He didn't know how long had passed as he trudged out from behind the mounds of snow kissed bushes, bushes that he could be thankful for as they had probably cushioned his fall.

Standing back on the path again he looked around.

"I should call this in he thought." And finally looked down at the Bobcat, the radio demolished in the wreckage. He pulled his cell phone out of his pocket.

"Fuck it!" He growled and gazed at the fragmented piece of uselessness now in his hand. He discarded it angrily to the floor and starred at the wounded Bobcat.

He crouched down and got a closer look at the broken ski, wondering what caused the crash.

"Well, you're not going anywhere! Are you buddy?" He said patting it on its now freezing cold hood, the fact that the engine was stone cold indicated to him that he'd been unconscious for a while. He sunk his hand back into the inviting warmth of his glove and was just about to stand back up when he noticed something attached to the rear of the ski. He brushed away the snow to reveal something metal, rusted in places and heavily scratched. As he looked closer and removed more of the snow he realised what it was.

"A bear trap?"

He grabbed a palm full of snow, as if to make a snowball and then pressed it to his throbbing head, the pain eased a little, but the knot on his head was the least of his worries. He stood up and with the rapid beating of his heart almost thumping out of his chest. He matched those thumps with his footsteps and used his panic stricken heart to spur him on towards the cabins.

CHAPTER 32

The warm glow of the fire and the marijuana that had settled in her system was enough to make Mia doze. Her one good eye that was functional began to flutter as if to close, as she sat wrapped up in the fur skins on her new favourite armchair.

"This is Miss Crystal!" Dustin brayed enthusiastically, which woke her from her drifting. He held the trading card of a lovely platinum blonde beauty, her siliconed implants standing firm and to attention as they burst from the V of a luxurious red sequinned gown, with long white evening gloves that rose up to meet her elbows.

"She's the manager of Sebastian Churchill. D'you remember me showing you him?" He added.

"Yeah, sure!" Mia shrugged consumed with boredom.

"This is him." Dustin said showing her the card anyway, before laying them back down on the wooden floor below. The cards were all spread out, as he sat crossed legged like a child so excited to share his world with someone else, even if that someone else wasn't interested. At least it gave him an excuse to talk about a passion of his.

"Yep, there he is!" Mia said unenthusiastically and rolled her eyes at the rotund blonde haired man, with unpleasant warts peppered on his smug looking face.

"Next up is 'Magnificent' Johnny Midnight!" He said flashing the next card in her line of sight. This time her eyes lit up and she took the card from him.

"Oh, Hello!" She gushed, obviously liking what she saw.

"Yeah, I thought you might like this one!" Dustin scoffed shaking his head "Is it the sleek dark hair, his chiseled bone structure or the bubbling rows of abs you're looking at?" He continued laughing.

"All of the above!" She whistled.

He snatched the card back from her grip before she lost all control and drooled on it.

"Don't bend it, sheesh!" Dustin said checking that she hadn't creased it in anyway before safely placing it next to Miss Crystal.

"Get a life Dust!" She whined.

"This is my life!" He said staring at her with all sincerity in the world attached to the words.

She rolled her eyes again and looked down at her novel that sat on the arm of the chair. She sighed in frustration, really wanting to carry on reading the story, as there were only a couple of chapters remaining and she could hardly wait to find out how it ends. But with only having the one functional eye, it made it difficult for her to focus on things and the fact her glasses had been broken meant that there was no way she'd be finishing the book anytime soon.

"And this one is the pièce de résistance of my collection! It's limited edition and my favourite pro wrestler of all time... 'The American Man' Randy Rogan!" Dustin announced as if he was heralding his arrival to the ring. "You have heard of Randy Rogan?" He added.

"Everyone's heard of Randy Rogan!" She snapped back.

The door burst open and the violent onslaught of wind forced snow into the cabin, causing the two to shield their faces, unable to see anything but the gust of snow. The fire flickered rapidly behind them under the unrelenting glacial gale and Dustin's cards swept up into the air and were sent fluttering everywhere.

"My cards!" He shouted.

"Screw your cards!" Mia yelled back "It's going to blow the fire out! C'mon on!"

They both ran into the flurry and with all their might forced the door shut and locked the bolt across.

"Oh, would you look at that!" Dustin groaned.

His cards now in complete disarray on the floor. He scuttled down onto the floor and began gathering them up.

Mia sauntered back over to her chair and sank back down into its cozy refuge.

"What the hell happened to Max?" Mia said, finally realising he hadn't returned after at least fifteen minutes.

"He's probably planning something somewhere." Dustin replied setting his cards back out on the floor in numerical order.

"Yeah, you're probably right." Mia shrugged entombing herself back in the warmth and comfort of the fur skins, almost becoming submerged in them, only her eyes and top of her head could be seen now.

"There we go!" Dustin said having all the cards back in their place and slotting Randy Rogan at the end of them.

"Did you know that Randy Rogan was World Heavyweight Champion six times?"

"Is that so?" Mia yawns and her eye starts to flicker again, this time not bothering to fight against the slumber.

"Yeah! He even won championships in Canada and Japan..."

His words trailed off as they all became fused together in a tumble weed of words.

Blah, blah, blah she thought.

Dustin's shape had become hazy to her in her woozy state, framed by amber of the fire behind him he was soon replaced by the ripped physique of Johnny Midnight, the wrestler on the card that Mia had been so infatuated with earlier. She smirked in her sleepy state and watched as he gyrated in front of her in his small spandex trunks. The glow of the fire glistening on his protruding abdominals that seem to dance along with his snake like hips.

Something wandered across her distorted slumbering mirage and her eye flickered open again, the glare of the fire seemed to have gone, but the warmth remained. Her vision returned and she focused on Dustin still hunched over the cards, and still babbling about the life and times of Randy Rogan.

It wasn't until her vision returned properly that she saw that something was indeed blocking the light. The gargantuan mass of one Beau Tooth behind the oblivious Dustin.

She murmured something from underneath her fur skinned sanctuary, but the words could not be heard properly.

The cumbersome axe was heaved up over his scarred and uneven skull, the golden glow of the fire flashed against the bloodstained head of his weapon. She tried to scream but couldn't, she sank even further down into the fur skins, hoping and praying that this beast had not yet seen her.

"Did you say something, Mia?" Dustin said looking up at her. The axe hurtled down with vicious ferocity and carved him in half, his lifeless body fanning out in two like the petals of a blooming flower. Blood erupted from his remains like some human volcano, dousing everything with speckles of his vital fluid. As the last of the gore left Dustin's remains he collapsed to the floor next to his collection of precious trading cards, dots of blood dripped on the cards of Miss Crystal, Johnny Midnight and Randy Rogan.

Mia sat frozen, scared for her very life, but with the slightest of hope that the killer did not know she was there nestled in the mass of fur skins. Beau Tooth glanced down at his handy work and smiled a sickening sadistic smile, his fat tongue caressing his broken tusks. He lifted the axe that had taken yet another life and inspected it almost salivating. Slowly he brought it in close to his face, maybe to get a closer look, maybe those dark eyes of Satan weren't too good after all and Mia may still have a chance at survival.

She remained perfectly still, she hadn't even noticed that she was now holding her breath.

Mia fought back the retching that convulsed in her chest and throat as she watched the horrendous sight of Beau Tooth licking the dripping viscera from the edge of the blade and tasting it. His sockets were too dark to make out what his eyes were doing, but Mia thought that maybe he would have closed his eyes and savoured the flavour like some French sommelier would taste a fine wine.

Suddenly Beau Tooth strode away, out of her view. Her eye was wide and she tried to look around for his whereabouts, but she could no longer see him. She could no longer hear his heavy nasal breaths, like those of a congested boar. She swallowed hard and slowly and quietly she rose from her nest. She turned gradually taking in all the dark corners of the room, she saw nothing in those shadows as the light from the fire illuminated furniture and painted their shadows up on the walls. The eyes of the mounted animals looked down at her, fire in their eyes that seem to warn her.

But to no avail as she turned all the way around there he was, standing behind her, toying with her and waiting for that moment for her to turn around.

With a swipe of the axe he scalped her.

Her flesh and dark mass of hair flew through the air and landed on the floor. Mia screamed. She fell from the armchair and struggled to untwine herself from under the mass of heavy fur skins, she crawled over the bloody remains of Dustin with tears now streaming out of her eye. Tooth grabbed her ankle and she turned to face him instinctively kicking at him. He let go for a moment and she crawled onwards, but he was back on her again grabbing her by the scruff of her sweatshirt and effortlessly lifting her up off the ground. He seemed to smirk at her before slamming her down onto the floor face first. The bearskin rug doing little to soften the blow and the air left her body on impact. She found herself in front of the fire and grabbed at the poker stand that stood next to her, but all she managed to do was knock it over, the tools falling agonisingly out of reach.

He grabbed her ankle again, this time the grip of his chunky frost bitten hand was unbreakable. She cried into the fire place her tears looking like tiny balls of flame as they trickled down her cheeks. He was now squatting over her, she could feel his thick breath on the nape of her neck and again she felt the urge to vomit. With nothing else left to do she blunged her hand into the flames and grabbed a log from that was still ignited. She suppressed the pain that she felt and adrenaline hurtled through her body. She managed to turn and swipe the flaming log at him. His shirt caught fire and he backed off dabbing at the fire with his hand. Mia staggered to her feet, blood dripping down her face from her exposed skull.

"Eat this you bastard!" She yelled and swiped at him again. He grabbed her hand and took the log from her grip, her hand was now severely burnt and fear consumed her face, she knew it was over.

He smiled at her, his shirt still burning, cotton fusing with flesh, his beard alight now too, the smell of his damp hair smouldering was sickening to her, but she no longer saw the benefit of vomiting, she would take it all to her grave. He gripped the burning log in his hand, he cared not that his flesh was now blistering under the heat of the flame. Without a second thought he heinously pushed it into Mia's snivelling face and held it there until her body went limp.

The smouldering log burnt straight through her flesh and blood blended with the fire creating a devilish crimson fury of flame.

CHAPTER 33

Something woke Jessica from her slumber. She sat up and her eyes blinking rapidly as she tried to focus. Had a large sound woke her or was it something in a dream? She couldn't say, but she was awake now and she got out of bed. She was still naked from her virginal voyage into love making and she shivered as goosebumps rose on top of goosebumps. There was a draft seeping its way into the cabin from somewhere. Quickly she grabbed Quack's discarded SCU Chess Club sweatshirt and put it on, the task was accompanied by the quivering sound of her lips, displaying just how cold she was.

"What time is it?" She asked herself and tiptoed barefoot across the chilly floorboards towards her cellphone that stood silent on its speaker having come to the end of its romantic playlist long ago.

The time on the screen showed 21:35, 25% battery life (It hadn't charged as expected) and no signal.

"I've been asleep for two hours!" She gasped and retrieved her underwear that had fallen to the floor during their moment of passion. She quickly slipped them on and let the large sweater consume her small frame, it hung to her mid thigh and covered up anything she didn't want anyone to see.

"Maybe he came back and saw that I was asleep and didn't want to disturb me. He's probably gone downstairs and joined the others?" She pondered and nodding thinking that this was indeed what had happened.

She suddenly heard a loud bang.

The sound carried through the whole of the wooden cabin shaking its very foundations.

Was this the same sound that awoke her from her sleep? She didn't know.

She stood frozen for a minute or two, waiting to hear the sound again. It didn't disappoint. It was the slamming of the front door. She knew this because it was the same sound that announced Rob's departure from the cabin only one day ago.

"What are they doing down there?" She asked herself.

Jessica slipped on some thick comfortable socks and stepped out onto the landing. The cold breeze hit her immediately and seem to whistle its chilling whine all-around her. She shuddered and let the long sleeves of the sweatshirt cover her hands and then she wrapped them around her torso like she was wearing a straight-jacket, but the sweatshirt smelt like Quack and that was comforting to her.

She cautiously walked across the landing towards the stairs. She noticed that Sophie's supper was still sitting outside her bedroom door and thought to herself that she must really be taking this break up with Rob hard.

She could see that the bathroom door was a jar and the lights were off indicating to her that it wasn't in use, so she felt no need to look inside. That slamming of the door again stopped her in her tracks for a moment and then another gust of cold chilling wind struck her causing her to shudder again.

"What the hell is going on?"

She knew something wasn't quite right, she could feel it, she could sense it, she could smell it.

As she reached the top of the stairs her nose contorted from some awful, nauseating aroma, something had been burning. It was a smell that she could not fathom, she had never smelt anything so sickening before in her life. The long sleeve of the sweatshirt immediately covered her nose and mouth, she could no longer stand it.

She reached the stairs and looked down into the main room. The lights were off, but the fire raged on and illuminated the room, forcing peculiar shaped shadows onto the wall and ceiling, they seemed to dance and gyrate as the flames quivered from the constant onslaught from the penetrating wind. She stood at the top of the stairs looking down into the eeriness and called out "You guys?"

She waited but the only response was the whistling of the wind.

"Are you guys down there?" She called again. The door slammed again and made her jump. She began to step down the staircase slowly, the room opening up in front of her. The flames reflecting in the trophies eyes were creepy to her and seemed to follow her as she entered.

"Hello?" She called again looking around, hugging herself tightly "If this is some sort of joke, it's not funny!" She yelled before shuddering again with that cold wind that had brought with it a pile of snow that now lay in the entrance. She quickly moved over towards it and using all of her might managed to push the door shut. She bolted it and breathed a sigh of relief. She tried the light switch, but nothing. She moved towards the kitchen area where the telephone was and picked up the receiver, the line was dead.

"What is going on here?" She asked herself and gently hung the receiver back in place looking round the room in confusion, as a courtroom of taxidermy seemingly judged her.

CHAPTER 34

The look of dread and shock was frozen on the deceased face of Dustin as he was dragged unceremoniously through fresh snow, then through grimy slush where two ski marks had cut through the snow and earth. Beau Tooth panted heavily as he let go of Dustin's ankle. His breath carrying into the air like smoke bellowing from a locomotives chimney. The beast was tired as he surveyed his old wooden sledge that had the bodies of his victims casually piled up on top of each other. Conspicuous by their absence was the bodies of Elroy Pascoe and Robert Guy who had already been retrieved by Tooth a day earlier.

He grabbed Dustin's lifeless corpse and nonchalantly reunited him with his friends, throwing him on top the pile of bodies. The gaping Max, the broken in half Sophie, the faceless Mia and the minced mass of Quack's remains.

He trudged slowly round to the front of the sledge and searched for the chain that was attached to it, it had sunken in the snow and he fished it out with his blistering dark hands, that no longer felt that relentless bite from the Canadian winter, seemingly immune to any feeling at all. His hands were scarred heavily, and had been gnawed on by several winters of the past, making them appear black and lifeless. It is quite possible that this was reflected in the brutes heart. Perhaps that to hung lifeless in his chest, scarred by time, black and paralysed. No longer able to feel anything. Those pleasant summer memories making love with his wife on a picnic blanket in the middle of the woods, or pushing his children on the tyre swing that he built them. Helping to build the cabins where the lumberjacks lived. The first tree he cut down. Perhaps even his wedding day or the birth of his children.

There must be no memory of these things within him or he would not do the despicable things he does.

A heart without love is like a broken pencil, pointless.

He stopped, his cauliflower ears pricking, hearing something. He dropped the chain to the floor and listened intently.

A smile caressed his chapped maw and licked his lips with anticipation, drool dripping into his disheveled beard that fluttered in the wind like a flag on a mast.

He heard her voice, she called out to her friends from the cabin and those dark eyes seemed to light up with purpose. It would appear that this winters hunt was not yet over.

CHAPTER 35

That smell again attacked her nostrils causing her face to contort. That foul burning aroma, the stench of scorched flesh. She winced as she looked around confused, it was then that she noticed the wrestling cards left discarded and in disarray on the floor.

"Dustin wouldn't go anywhere without his cards." She told herself as she approached them and slipped on the hardwood flooring. She looked down to see what she had slipped on. The floor looked almost black in places, something had been spilt, but she couldn't see what it was.

"Oooh! Gross!" She murmured before she sat down into that oh so comfortable armchair that her friend Mia had claimed. She lifted up her foot to get a closer look at what sticky substance had attached itself to her sock. Her fingers touched it and it stuck to them, the consistency of syrup.

"What is that?" She asked herself, looking at her stained fingertips.
The fire flickered and without the assault from the wintery gale, it brightened up the room a little, illuminating the substance trickling down her fingertips.
Blood.

"Oh my God!" She gasped and frantically wiped it on Quack's sweatshirt.

"What the hell is going on?" She shivered this time through fear and anxiety not of the cold, she stood up and backed away from the puddle of blood that was now visible on the floor, now surrounding the trading cards.

"Hello!" She shouted as loud as she could, tears started to ease their way into eyes, blurring her vision "Hello!"

But there was no answer and the cabin stood still and silent, like they had never even been there.

As she stepped back not able to take her eyes of the blood and wondering in the back of her mind who it belonged to, she trod on something, it squelched underfoot and she slipped falling awkwardly backwards and hitting her head on the unforgiving thick floorboards. She was out for what could have been seconds, but may have felt like minutes, hours or even days. And with her head full of stupor she sat up dazed and confused and for the second time she felt that horrendously chilling shiver fluctuate through her body. She rubbed the back of her head, a *Looney Tunes* lump was there to greet her fingertips and she winced and then shivered once more. She turned to see that the door was open again.

"How long was I out?" She asked herself and glanced around.

She remembered that she had slipped and then the blood again made her eyes saucer.

She looked around for what she slipped on and put her hand on it. It felt like soft bristles to her touch and she wondered what it was, she picked it up and the horror struck her and struck hard. In her hand was Mia's scalp, the beautiful dark fibres clung to a flap of skin and flesh that dripped blood onto the floorboards. She screamed and threw it away. Then the tears came for real, she hugged her knees and rocked back and forth for a moment.

"What is going on? What is going on?" She repeated through sniffs and snivels. Then the realisation of what had happened here, the amount of blood, the scalp, her friends missing. They must be... "Dead!" She whispered.

"I've got to get out of here!" She cried and was up and rummaging through Quack's Parker for his van keys, she found them and quickly jammed her blood stained socks into her boots. Then slid her red Parker on quickly and with a quick swipe she zipped it up as she darted out into the blistering cold, stuffing the keys into her pocket.

She trudged through the deep snow towards Quack's van as quickly as she could. The van sat helpless in a few feet of snow, like a dead slug surrounded in salt.

The cold stabbed at her exposed legs and she wondered whether leaving the house was such a good idea.

She reached the van and instinctively tried the door, it was locked of course. She rummaged in her pocket and retrieved the bunch of keys, she stopped to look at the keyring, a family portrait staring back at her. Quack and his mother and his little sister Agnes smiling at her, trapped in a pleasant memory. Tears began to build up in her eyes again, still really not knowing what had happened there tonight, but knowing enough that it wasn't good.

Something caught her eye back near the cabin, something glittered and it got her attention enough to stop what she was doing and look back. It was the head of an axe that was winking at her in the darkness and there by the entrance of the cabin stood Beau Tooth.

"Oh my God!" She gasped, the words almost vomiting from her mouth as she unfortunately dropped the keys into the snow.

"No!"

Tooth saw this as his opening and sailed through the deep snow like a ship coming in to harbour, the axe raised in front of him as to not hinder his rhythm.

Jessica dived into the cold snow in search of the car keys. "The keys! The keys!" She whined in anguish, all the time keeping her head on a swivel as Tooth came ever closer like a Great White Shark that has detected the blood of a wounded creature.

"Get the fuck away from me!" She screamed, feeling the metal loop of the keys in her fingertips, before finally clutching them tightly in her hand.

"Leave me alone! Leave me alone!" She cried.

Tooth just grinned at her and said nothing, clouds of air spouting from his nostrils like some angry bull.

The key slid into the lock and it opened, pushing back a mound of snow that had settled against the door. She yanked the keys back out and dived into the drivers seat slamming the door shut behind and immediately locking it. Her hands shaking, red and cold. She looked out the window for the menace, but he was no longer there. She looked out all the windows, all around her they were fogged up, but she saw nothing. She knew she couldn't waste time worrying about his whereabouts and she jammed the keys into the ignition. The engine kicked in and a loud purring cough filled the air. The headlights illuminated the dark cabin out in front and she smiled, letting out a sigh of relief, but then the lights flickered and the engine coughed again before it died.

"No, no, no, no!" She shrieked trying in vain to turn the engine over.

"Shit!"

She sat in the drivers seat and suddenly felt like she wasn't alone. The van swayed slightly as though it had taken on some extra weight. Slowly she climbed over the drivers seat and into the centre of the van where she sat. She felt a little safer away from the windows, but her head on the swivel again at every slight noise. She clutched her knees and brought them in tightly to meet her chest again and held her breath.

There seemed to be no sound for the longest time, nothingness had consumed the Maple Woods as she waited. She didn't know what she was waiting for. For her attacker to strike or Dustin and Max to jump up the window serenading her with 'Gotcha's'. Nothing would giver her more pleasure if it were to be the latter.

There was the sound of something squeaking on the roof, she looked up and shuddered, still holding her breath and praying that it would all just go away. Trying to remember the lords prayer, but failing.

Then there was a scraping sound of metal on metal, almost hypnotic and haunting, as something was dragged across the grooves on the roof. Jessica buried her head into the thick softness of the Parker and clamped herself tightly into a ball, the way that an armadillo might do to evade a predator. The noise stopped and her head surfaced, tears staining her face as she looked all around, listening.

Slam came the axe of Beau Tooth down hard on the roof, it reverberated the van, shaking violently under the blow. Another and the axe cut through the roof.

Jessica screamed madly as more blows from the axe rained down on the roof, churning up the meagre metal that topped the van.

Jessica attempted to escape through the sliding door and the axe adjusted its technique, as it came hurtling through the window.

She screamed again as she was showered in broken glass and the axe head just missing her face by inches. She fell backwards on to the floor of the van and looked up. Dozens of gapping holes were now carved into the roof and the fluttering of snowflakes fell down around her. Through the holes she could see him moving around, then he lent forward and gazed at her through the one of the holes and grinned, saliva joining the falling snowflakes. He laughed in a boar like booming grunt its velocity carried through the woods and amplified.

Fearing that it would be the last sound she ever heard, she screamed again and Tooth suddenly took on a second wind and started to attack the rest of the windows with the head of his axe. More glass imploded, smothering her in tiny shards.

Her poor face glistened with moisture, it was difficult to make out what were tears, snowflakes or glass.

Feeling the time was right, she opened the sliding side door and dropped out into the snow before heading back towards the cabin. She used the pathway that Tooth had carved into the snow and was back at the cabin in no time at all. She looked behind her and saw him standing on the roof watching her as she slammed the door shut behind her. All she could hear now over her heavy gasps for air was his mocking laughter.

CHAPTER 36

The sound of roaring heinous laughter carried through the trees a sound that was so horrifying that it stopped Sheriff Russell in his tracks. It was like no sound that he had ever heard before and didn't wish to hear again if he were being completely honest. It scared him.

To him it was the sound of a viking's war cry or the growling of some rabid animal. His legs were aching and his joints were cold, he waited for a moment as the woods fell silent once more. He listened intently for that war cry again, hoping and praying that it would not come. It didn't.

He told himself that could mean one of two things. One, whatever foul depraved hellion made that sound had met its end, hopefully gruesomely.

Two, he was too late. He couldn't be too late, he wouldn't allow it and aching joints or not he would get there.

The light that acted as his beacon early on had faded which also dampened his hopes, but a soft flickering of amber still burned on and lead the way.

With his legs almost useless, like two cold cuts of meat hanging from a butchers hook, he urged them to carry on. He trudged on dragging his fatigued carcass onwards towards whatever unspeakable horrors were awaiting him.

CHAPTER 37

Jessica sat up against the locked door of the cabin, weeping and shaking, still trying to come to terms with what was actually happening.

"What's going on?" She weeped "I want to go home!"

She knew he would come for her, why wouldn't he?

He'd come.

Maybe running back to the cabin wasn't a wise move, she was cornered now. But it was instinct, human nature to head for the security of those four walls and a roof over our heads, giving us a false comfort.

She whined miserably wanting to move, knowing that she needed too, if she wanted to stay alive. But she couldn't, her body seemed to be shutting down, accepting her fate. Her legs were freezing and red raw, her face drenched with tears, there were broken shards of glass glistening in her hair, and her chest felt tight. It was if there was a weight on her, suffocating her. She wanted to run, but she felt paralysed by the fear to even attempt to do so.

"He's killed everyone, I know it!" She sniffed. But her eyes widened suddenly "Sophie!" She actually smiled "Sophie's been in her room all day!"

She hoisted herself up from the floor and ran towards the stairs. As her wet snow covered boot hit the first step there was a loud thud at the door which stopped her in mid stride.

He was here.

Thud!

She remained frozen.

Thud! Thud! Came the strikes on the door.

She swallowed hard and closed her eyes.

But still the strikes came, harder and faster, the sound of wood splintering. It was his axe hacking through the door.

She took a deep breath and actually thought that luck was on her side, it would take a long time for him to chop his way through the door single-handedly. In that time she could wake Sophie up and they could form a plan of escape.

No such luck, as the axe head suddenly appeared through a splintering of wood.

"No!" She shrieked and changed her course, now heading for the kitchen. Frantically she slid open drawers until the cutlery drawer tumbled out and fell to the floor, scattering forks, spoons and knives everywhere. She grasped the sharpest knife she could find and made a beeline for the door.

The hole had already doubled in size, big enough for Beau Tooth to slot his hand through and search blindly for the bolt. As his chunky misshaped hand lurked in she stabbed at it in a hysterical rage. The blade piercing the festering leathered skin again and again. When blood finally trickled from several stab wounds the hand recoiled back to the safety of the other side.

"Fuck you! You bastard!" Jessica cried and then ran for the stairs again. As she reached the top in what could have been a world record time, Tooth's hand appeared again. He ripped away at the bolt which gilded from the safety of its hole it had been resting in, and the door swung open.

Beau Tooth stood in the entrance, the wind blowing the snow around him, he looked like some ghostly apparition, here to take her soul. In a way that's exactly what he was.

There were no smiles on his ugly face this time. No playful look in his pitch black eyes. He'd been wounded by his prey and now it had to die.

They made eye contact for a few seconds and he glared at her, letting her know that playtime was indeed over.

She dashed across the landing and came to Sophie's room, she burst in and the room was empty.

"Sophie? No..." Realisation hit home that Sophie had gone too.

"Shit! Oh, God! Oh, No!" She teared up again and grasped the handle of the knife tightly in her clammy hands.

She headed back onto the landing and didn't know where to go for the best. She could hear his heavy footsteps falling on the stairs and the haunting sound of his axe walloping against each step as he dragged it behind him. He was taking his time, toying with his prey once more.

She darted into the bathroom and closed the door as quietly as she could and she looked for the key to lock it, but the key was not in its usual resting place, and the keyhole looked deformed and useless anyway. She thought of hiding and waiting until he passed, if he passed.

But where?

It was then that she turned around to see the toilet lathered in blood and viscera. It spilled onto the floor and surrounded it, seeping into the crevices of the tiles.

She clasped her hand around her face to stop her from screaming or vomiting, or maybe even both. She slowly approached the mess and peered into the bowl. In it was the tattered remains of Quack's favourite t-shirt.

"No, no, Quack! No!" She wept.

She really had fallen in love with Quack and just hours ago had spent such a beautiful time together, making great memories and maybe a future for themselves, which seemed like that could only take place now in another universe. Those moments of happiness were gone and she wondered whether she would ever feel happiness again.

Beau Tooth's heavy axe thumping the hardwood of the landing indicated he had arrived.

She looked around for somewhere to hide as the monotonous scrapping of his axe on the panels grew louder. She spotted the old style cast iron bath and hurried towards it as quietly as she could. She climbed inside and lay down. Her heart raced and she had to cup her hand over her nose and mouth so that he couldn't hear her heavy shaky breathes. She clutched the knife to her chest as she lay waiting, hoping he wouldn't come. Praying that if he did, he wouldn't see her.

The duet of axe and wood stopped abruptly. Slowly the door creaked open, he stood in the doorway looking in at the bathroom that was now as quiet as a crypt. She shook with fear as she saw his shadow form on the wall and seeped up eerily to the ceiling, almost filling the entire room.

He stood there surveying the room.

Jessica held her breath, for a moment it was as if she had stopped her own heart from beating.

He saw nothing and moved along, axe and wood singing its frightful cacophony again.

She breathed a sigh of relief that seemed to kickstart her heart again, and peered up over the side of the bathtub staring at the doorway. The sound of the axe dragging symphony decreased and then there was silence. Jessica slowly crept out of the bathtub and tiptoed to the door, she looked out onto the dark corridor and saw nothing, she heard nothing. She walked out from the doorway and headed for the stairs when her throat and neck suddenly felt very tight and she was yanked back with furious velocity.

She struggled and squirmed on the floor dropping the knife and instinctively trying to grab at whatever was around her throat.

She was pulled back again and lay on the floor, Tooth stood over her with a rope wrapped tightly in his hands.

Her eyes begged to breathe, but his black eyes stared back at her with nothingness. There was no remorse in those marbled eyes.

Jessica managed to work the fingers of her left hand between the rope and her throat, which gave her a lifeline. Small amounts of air were allowed in, she managed to grab the knife as he hoisted her up by the rope with ease and he weaved and knotted the rope behind her to form a noose-like knot. With her back to him and not knowing what he was doing she stabbed backwards blindly with the knife until it struck something, he growled like a wounded animal as the blade sunk into his thigh. In the struggle his grip loosened and he lost his footing falling into one of the rooms, Quack's room.

She landed on top of him, and came face to face with evil. She

228

screamed and tried to crawl away, the rope now loose enough for her to breathe.

Crawling towards the window, she tried to pull herself up on the widow ledge, but she felt that pull again and the rope was taut around her throat once more. She was spun around and then she dropped to her knees looking up at him. Her face started to change all manner of shades like the scales of a chameleon as she fought for life. The rough fibres of the rope burning her skin as it constricted around her windpipe, her eyes rolling back in her head as she gasped. He continued to wrap the rope around his gigantic mitts, it was obvious to her that he was enjoying what he was doing. Suddenly he winced and growled in discomfort again as the knife slid back out from the thigh it had been using as a sheath. He looked down to see her purple face smiling at him as she drove the knife through his work boot, piercing leather and flesh, it was enough to halt him. He growled angrily in pain and again his grip on the rope slackened. She pulled the knife back out of his foot and she stood up panting, a normal colour returning to her cheeks as she stared at him pointing the knife at the wounded boar.

"Leave me alone you bastard! Just leave me alone, God damn it!" She started to cry again "Please just leave me alone!" came a whisper as Beau Tooth straightened up and she found herself backed up against the window. With a powerful thrusting kick to her chest she was sent hurtling out of the window in a cascading shower of glass. The rope suddenly went taut again and this time she found herself hanging from the window unable to breathe once more. Beau Tooth stood at the window, framed in broken glass as he held the rope waiting to see her final breath. As she gagged and cried, gasping

229

for air she realised the knife was still tightly gripped in her hand. A strange thought entered her head, at that moment she thought that she could never do without this knife in her hand, her hand had taken this knife and it was part of her, an extension of her body. Its purpose was her survival. She began to swipe away above her head at the rope, her feet kicking against the cabin wall, searching for something to step on to and take off the pressure. Finally she felt the blade make contact with the rope and she began to hack at it rapidly in a sawing motion, the rope began to split, the fibres splaying out and when her weight became too much for it, finally it snapped and her body fell to the floor below. She lay there in the snow clutching the knife as air returned to her lungs again.

Beau Tooth looked down at her and Jessica raised her middle finger to meet his annoyed gaze. When he disappeared, she thought that she should probably do the same, so running on empty she ran, or tried to as best as she could. She screamed and yelled at the top of her voice, her vocal cords felt burnt after taking such tremendous punishment, but she had to try and alert someone, anyone.

She headed off into the woods and came face to face with a sledge full of her friends. She vomited and fell to her knees in the snow, no longer worrying or caring about how cold it was on her flesh, she cried.

The twisted corpses of her dear friends lay piled on top of each other, each one more gruesome than the next.

She vomited again. The heat of the cantaloupe coloured bile burnt through the snow rapidly and an awful aroma rose from its vapour.

She screamed. She screamed so loud and so long with everything she had left.

CHAPTER 38

Sheriff Russell bent over, his hands clasping his freezing thighs, as he tried to get his wind back. His body snapped back into place immediately when he heard a terrifying scream, the screaming of a girl.

"No!" He murmured and with his third or maybe his fourth wind kicking in, he bounded on.

He reached the cabin in the next few minutes of nonstop strides and removed his gloves, throwing them to the ground as he flicked the clasp out of place and slid his handgun out of its holster and held it in his grip. He glanced over and saw the van, dishevelled and destroyed, filled with holes like a skewered pig.

He moved towards the cabin, when the sound of the woodshed door swaying in the breeze caught his attention. He noticed blood spattered up against the door that swung back and forth in the breeze.

"Fuck!" He snarled and moved closer to the cabin.

It didn't take a detective to work out that the door had been forced, the huge hole in it was enough to tell him that. He crept into the cabin, the stench of burnt flesh attacked his red flaring nostrils and he sneered at it, but moved on. His gun out in front surveying the room like hundreds of exercises he had under-took in the police academy so many years ago. Checking all corners and watching his back, routine sequential stuff. He found nothing but more blood on the floor and what he first thought was some kind of dead animal. He knelt down, blood staining the knee of his trousers and poking at the thing on the floor with the end of his gun. His heart sank and his stomach rumbled with the sudden urge to lose his liquid lunch when he realised it was someones scalp. He left it alone and stood back up.

"What in God's name is going on here?"
He looked around and those open mouths of the hunters trophies protruding from the walls seemed to laugh at him. The fire dancing in their eyes as he stared at them all and he could have sworn that he had heard their hysterical laughter, mocking him for being too late.

"Too slow...too late!" He murmured as he gazed around at the laughing maws of racoons, wolverines, badgers and a timber wolves.

"No!" He told himself and headed for the stairs.
He crept up, handgun leading the way and he searched every room and found nothing, apart from the disgusting scene in the bathroom and the broken window in another, nothing.
He looked out of the broken window and asked himself "Where are the bodies?"
He looked down at the Jessica shape outline into the snow below and noticed that there were footsteps sprouting from it that headed towards Old Syrup. This gave him hope that there were still survivors and when he heard that scream again he looked out into those swaying trees that concealed all manner of secrets from him.

CHAPTER 39

Jessica ran through the trees as fast as she could, she could move a lot quicker through the centre of the woods as the mass cover of trees above had shrouded the floor from the majority of the fallen snow.

She panted heavily and rubbed at her throat that wore a deep burn and laceration around it like some fashionable choker.

She suddenly ran out of wood and found herself at the edge of Maple Lake, the frozen Old Syrup splayed out in front her. With a thick mist shrouding the lake and gentle flakes of continuous snow falling, it made it very difficult to see anything past the lake. She could not see the trees of Blackfoot that stood over yonder, nor could she see Fisherman's Island that sat in the middle of the lake.

She could see nothing.

The mist was thick and cold and it made her shudder as it coiled around her bare legs, she could hear nothing, it was an eery and peculiar atmosphere. Peering back over her shoulder she could see no sign of the monstrous Beau Tooth.

Could she have outrun him, lost him?

She called out into the mist as loud as her bruised and swollen larynx would allow, "Hello!" The word lingering for minutes as it echoed around the frozen lake, as if looking for an escape route itself.

There was nothingness for a few minutes and she sighed. A sigh of understanding that she would either die by an axe wielding maniac or the cold would get her first and she would freeze to death.

"There's nobody out here." She quivered "Why would there be!"

"Hello!" Came a reply, it was faint but it was there and her eyes lit up.

There was hope.

"Help! I'm here!" She called and the words danced around the lake again, almost ice skating on its frozen surface.

This time there was no reply and she cupped her hands around her mouth and began to call again, with everything she had.

"Hell..." was all she could muster when she felt the axe's sharp bit slam into her back, the metal sickeningly cracking her spinal cord as she fell to the frosty shore the axe protruding out from her spine. Beau Tooth stood quietly over her carcass before removing the axe in a serenade of tearing flesh and crunching bone.

CHAPTER 40

Sheriff Russell had quickened his pace after hearing the cry for help. But after several minutes of calling back and no response meeting his cold ears, his heart sank.

His quick footed dash had suddenly became a trot and then a lowly shuffle. He felt like crying, just giving up, handing over his badge and gun and crying. He'd failed and he was so tired. His whole body ached and he was so cold.

Snow had started to fall heavily again and he knew that it would soon cover any tracks that he could follow.

"Where the hell are the bodies?" Was a sentence he kept asking himself, he had seen enough blood, but no bodies, not one.

"Just what has happened here?"

Suddenly there was a flock of white breasted nuthatches that burst into the air, and cut through the snow smothered branches, forcing it to all fall around the startled Sheriff.

He realised that something had startled those birds and he moved on again towards the lake.

A scraping sound of metal on ice caused Jessica's weary eyelids to flicker and open. Her vision was blurry and her head woozy, pain shot through her freezing body as she started to stir. She saw the mist, it appeared heavier as if she was in the thick of it. Her stomach felt nauseated, almost like travel sickness. She realised she was moving.

As she focused, she saw the ice of Old Syrup below and the back end of two rusted up old ski's that cut into the ice as it moved slowly along.

"A sledge?" She spluttered quietly to herself, try to get her brain to function. She smiled for a second thinking that she had been saved and then the smile disappeared as she turned to see the face of Quack, his features frozen in time like a screaming fossil.

"No!" She murmured and she tried to move. It was then that she noticed that she was on Beau Tooth's sledge of death with the dead mutilated corpses of her friends. She saw all their faces glaring at her, almost blaming her and accusing her.

"No, no, no!" She cried and tried to pull herself out of the heavy blanket of flesh.

The sledge came to a halt and Beau Tooth turned around to see Jessica crawling out of the pile of human remains and dropping onto the ice. He dropped the chain that he used to pull along the sledge and picked up his axe that was resting on top of the bodies.

Jessica crawled helplessly on the ice back towards the shore which was now a long way away. Snow fell on the ice as she turned her aching body around to face the reaper once again, who was yet again stalking her with an axe in his hands.

"Go on then!" She shouted at him "Do it!"

He was taken aback by such a request, nobody had ever asked him to kill them before. But she had literally had enough.

"Do it you fucking moron! I said Do it!" Her words exploded out of her and echoed for miles. If anyone was on her trail to save her they would have surely heard that and that's what she wanted.

She wasn't a stupid girl, she knew exactly what she was doing. He lifted the axe over his head and brought it crashing down with all his might, but she rolled out of the way and the axe smashed through the ice. Beau Tooth looked shocked as ice cracked around him and he fell into the cold unforgiving waters of Old Syrup.

The ice broke underneath her body and she too was submerged into the cold dark depths below the ice.

"Hello!" Came the call from Sheriff Russell at the bank, looking out into the misty nothingness. He looked down at the snow that covered the thick layer of ice, it made it very difficult to see where the lake started and the shore ended.

"I could have sworn I heard her call again?" He said to himself as he gazed out into nothing.

In the distance he heard the weeping and wailing of police sirens and he turned to see blue and red lights dancing through the trees.

"Sheriff?" He heard the voice of his Deputy echoing through the woods, through an amplifying megaphone "Are you out there, Sheriff?" it came again.

"I'm here!" He yelled back.

He sat down on the shore and suddenly was over come with emotion.

"C'mon, Pat! Get it out your system. Can't let them see you like this." He snivelled.

He cried and mucus ran down to meet his moustache, he wiped at his face with the sleeve of his jacket and shook his head.

"Those poor kids. Where are those poor fucking kids?"

He asked the question and knew immediately he didn't have the answer. What would he tell their parents? What would he write up in

237

the report about all of this? He shook his head and at that moment he felt like a complete failure. It was then that he felt the same pain and anguish that his predecessor must have felt and knew exactly what the report would say.

"More missing people."

In a gasp of cold air Jessica rose from the hole in the ice, her face blue and shuddering like a pneumatic drill. She clawed at the ice, digging her fingernails into it to pull herself out of an icy grave. In the distance she saw the blue and red lights shimmying through the mist, a smile caressed her dark blue lips and she whispered "I-I-I'm o-over h-h-here!"

She coughed and spluttered "I-It's o-okay!" She said a little louder "I'm s-s-safe now, they're h-h-here." She smiled and actually laughed as she shivered and pulled herself halfway out of the water.

"I-I-I'm..." She attempted to shout and her eyes grew wide as she was dragged back down into those cold dark waters.

The water thrashed around for a few moments and bubbles rose up and popped on the surface before the lake was calm again.

CHAPTER 41

Sheriff Russell sat on his sofa with his bare feet submerged in a bowl of warm water, a thick blanket wrapped around his shoulders as if he were some kind of monarch.

Holly hurried in with a bowl of hot chicken soup and handed it to him.

"Here now, you eat all this up. It'll do you good." She said smiling at him and rubbing his back lovingly.

"Thanks." He said and as he looked up at her, their eyes met and he started to cry. She took the soup bowl from him and placed it on the coffee table, then she embraced him.

"I wish I could make it go away, Pat. I really do."

"I just wish I could have saved them." He snivelled back.

"Is there no sign of them? Not any of them?"

He shook his head "They're out there combing the woods right now. But they won't find anything. Just like Windwood never found anything."

She rubbed his back again and wiped away his teary eyes.

"Shall I go and get you a drink?"

"Yeah!"

"Coffee?"

"Yeah, just make sure it's really Irish."

She left with a parting kiss to his raw and chapped cheek. He looked around the living room, it was then that he took in his surroundings, in the hour he'd been back he had been in a complete daze. He looked at the laptop that sat on the coffee table next to the chicken soup, the bright screen hurt his eyes as he bent down to retrieve the inviting bowl of warmness. He started to slurp it up like he'd never eaten in his life before. It felt good to him, calming as it passed down his throat and warmed his belly. He turned to the television, and ice skating was on. He rolled his eyes. Holly loved figure skating and watched it whenever it was on.

He went back to his soup and heard the whistling of the kettle from the kitchen and then the commentator on the television made a throwaway remark for the current performance that had a tiny Chinese girl tiptoeing across the screen.

"*How fabulous she looks. It's so easy for her like she's just walking across that ice...*"

Those words hit a gong in his head and his eyes widened, he dropped the bowl and its contents to the floor, chicken soup spilling out everywhere.

"Is something wrong?" Holly cried as she ran in from the kitchen.

Sheriff Russell was leant over the laptop quickly typing away at the keys.

"What's going on?" She asked, he cut her off with an aggressive shushing noise as he came to what he was searching for. On the screen were the words...

Does The Blackfoot Exist?

A Report by Zoologist, Professor Felix Cumberbatch

"What is it?" Holly cried again shaking his shoulders.

He turned to her with a newfound fire in his eyes "I know where they are!"

CHAPTER 42

Snow fell in abundance that night on Maple Falls. It's motive to cover up all the dark deeds that had taken place, smothering it with tranquil layers of harmless snow.

Precautions had already taken place, Mother Nature covering it all up again, with the wailing of the wind, a wall of falling snow and a thick mist that settled around Old Syrup.

But if you listened carefully you could just about make out the horrid sound of metal scraping on ice.

THE END...

OTHER WORK AVAILABLE

NOVELS

Monster Home
Dinner Party
Vatican: Angel of Justice
Vatican: Retribution
Blood Stained Canvas
Maple Falls Massacre
Fear Trigger
Welcome to Crimson
Monster Meals

COMING SOON

Vatican: Unholy Alliance

Visit the website at www.djbwriter.co.uk

Follow author Daniel J.Barnes on social media
@DJBWriter on Facebook, Instagram & Twitter.

Proud to be part of the Eighty3 Design family. For all your website and graphic design needs.

www.eighty3.co.uk

Printed in Great Britain
by Amazon